Now that her brother Charles is happily married, Beatrice has time to take stock of her situation. Almost thirty, she is ready for a household of her own and a husband to share it with. But so far, Mr. Right has not appeared, only a profusion of Mr. Wrongs. Will she ever find a man who makes her heart race, such as that of the heroines in the romance novels she loves to read?

It is a dark and stormy night when a mysterious drenched Scotsman appears on the doorstep of Godshollow. Could this be the man of her dreams? Or has a terrible nightmare just begun? And how can she tell the difference, caught as she is in the midst of so much conflicting advice? Can she trust her heart to know the truth?

Godshollow Claimed
Copyright © 2021 Catherine Price
ISBN: 978-1-4874-3071-9
Cover art by Martine Jardin

Published by eXtasy Books Inc or
Devine Destinies, an imprint of eXtasy Books Inc

Look for us online at:
www.eXtasybooks.com or www.devinedestinies.com

GODSHOLLOW CLAIMED

BY

CATHERINE PRICE

DEDICATION

For anyone who never thought they could; we can.

PROLOGUE: 1649

"Incoming!"

The cry could barely be heard over the thundering approach of Cromwell's men. Even the trees in the forest opposite Godshollow seemed to move as the soldiers marched ever closer to the castle.

Lord Fraser turned to his wife. "It's time," he told her firmly.

"I can't," she whispered back, tears in her eyes.

Fraser took her by the shoulders and looked her straight in the eye. "Ye must," he implored.

"I won't," the woman wailed anew. "I've already lost a son. I won't lose a husband as well."

Pain gripped Fraser's chest as he thought of his only child. "I know, blossom. But think o' the bairn. Connor's memory *must* endure. Take Jamie and go tae Scotland, I still have some family left there. Ma brother, Montgomery, moved back tae Cromarty. He'll take ye in."

"But this is our home! We built it. You earnt this with years of service to the country. They can't take it away."

"I dunnae think they care about ownership now. We stood by the king, we're the enemy. There isnae a way we can defeat Cromwell, but by God will we fight. I'll challenge those bastards until ma dying breath, but I'll die a happy man if I know yer safe." He kissed his wife passionately, holding her for what he knew would be the last time. "Go, lass," he whispered. He pressed a gentle kiss on the forehead of the crying baby in the woman's arms.

Fraser stepped back and pulled a hidden lever. The book-case next to him was released from the wall with a quiet click, revealing a small passage. "They willnae know ye were even here."

Fraser drank in one last look of his wife before the secret door closed. He quickly heaved a heavy table in front of the false case — he didn't trust Cromwell's men not to search the place. He couldn't let them find the hidden escape route.

He ran out to the hallway and into the chaotic racing of the servants as the men prepared themselves for battle. Agatha and Jamie marked the last of the women and children to be evacuated.

Fraser strode purposefully through the crowd and made his way to the ramparts. He felt resigned. He knew they couldn't remove themselves from the war indefinitely, but he'd be damned if he wasn't going to give these Roundheads a hell of a fight.

He looked out over his grounds and saw the first of the soldiers appear from within the foliage. The footmen formed a barrier around the castle, spears pointed out defensively.

From somewhere within the encroaching army, a man on horseback trotted into the courtyard. Coming to a stop in front of his men, he pulled a piece of paper from his bag and laid his other hand on his sword.

"Lord Fraser Mackenzie," the man shouted up at the castle. He didn't wait for a response but began to read. "You are under arrest for loyalties to the former King, Charles Stuart, and his young son of the same name. We have orders to take you to the tower of London."

"Ye can try," Fraser called back. He rattled his sword provocatively between the merlons, backed by a line of men, some with bows, some with improvised projectiles. A heart-warming bellow of agreement sounded from those within the reach of his voice. When he had taken on his staff five years before, he had worried that the Englishmen would struggle to accept a Scottish nobleman — despite his twenty years serving the English Crown and Parliament. However, the men had surprised him, taking him and his family into their hearts and serving him loyally.

"Very well," the horseman replied curtly. Then he turned his horse about and trotted back to the rear of his army.

Coward, Fraser thought disgustedly. Willnae even fight. Well, I'll show him how a real man leads his men.

"*Buaidh no Bàs!*" He cried the ancient Celtic words, holding his claymore aloft. *Victory or death*. The men around him began to shout and cheer, though odds were, even after all this time spent living with a Scotsman, they had no idea what the foreign words meant. "Make ready!" Fraser instructed in English, leaving them with no doubts as to his intentions.

The archers stepped forward. Longbow strings were pulled back, arrows pointed at the enemy. Metal tips glinted in the sunlight.

For a moment, everything stilled. As though the world had come to a stop, men stood like statues frozen in time.

Fraser took a deep breath. "*Fire!*" he shouted.

A hail of arrows darkened the sky and began to fall upon the victims below. Blood covered the ground in a scarlet blanket. The bodies of the slain fell next to the objects that struck them — bricks, wood, chairs, tables, and anything else that hadn't been nailed down. The inhabitants of the castle used anything to keep up the assault, however amateur, whilst the archers prepared the next volley.

Recovering from this first attack, the hostiles began their assault. Soon arrows were flying in every direction and men were beginning to clash in a fierce mêlée.

All around him, Fraser's men were falling. He watched as the army brought forth a battering ram with which to break down the doors. He raced to the courtyard, calling to his men to maintain the bombardment from the battlements.

He joined the group of men standing defensively around their makeshift barricade. The doors were beginning to shake as the heavy thud of the wooden ram resounded. They would be through before very long.

"Let's give them hell, lads," Fraser shouted.

At a loud crack, wood splinters scattered in every direction. Men shouted as they poured through the now open entrance, their shouts soon replaced by the clang of metal swords.

The courtyard was quickly strewn with dead men from both sides.

Fraser fought as hard as he could. A skilled swordsman, he was able to defend himself. But as he saw the numbers of his men begin to dwindle, he knew their cause was lost. He had only a handful of men left. These few were quickly surrounded by a group of Roundheads.

He watched as the horse-riding noble who'd first addressed him slowly entered the courtyard, a sickeningly smug look on his face.

"Submit, Lord Fraser. You know we've won. Surely enough blood has been spilt."

Fraser spat at the ground in front of the horse and swore in Gaelic. "I willnae submit," he announced defiantly. "This is ma land. Ye may cut me down, but this will nae ever be yer land."

The parliamentarian looked down at Fraser with a contemptuous smirk. He waved his hand airily and sighed, as though dealing with an unruly child. "Surrender, Fraser," he said in a bored tone. "If you come with us, I'll spare the remainder of your measly band of rebels. If you continue to fight, it will be to the death."

Fraser looked to his men. They'd been with him for a long time. They were his good friends. He knew their wives and families. They'd served him dutifully. He couldn't ask any more of them. But they surprised him with their response.

"To the death!" they cried in unison. One of the men pulled a hatchet from his belt and sent it hurtling through the air. The weapon came to a stop in the chest of the horseman.

A bloody battle ensued as Fraser and his men dispatched as many of the parliamentarians as they could. The skirmish was brief but brutal. The last thing Fraser knew was the feel of a sharp blow to his chest. An arrow protruded from his tunic. He watched with morbid fascination as the green and blue tartan turned to red. A soldier stood in front of him, sword raised.

"With ma blood," Fraser said as boldly as he was able. "I declare this land as forever belonging to the Mackenzies."

Then the final stroke fell.

CHAPTER ONE: 1821

Rain lashed heavily against the large bay window. The curtains were drawn wide as Beatrice peered out into the ferocious, storm that was causing havoc to the courtyard.

She found something irresistible about watching a storm. A tempest was so powerful and chaotic—and it was one of her favourite things.

Not to mention that being able to watch from within God-shollow was a miracle. She still couldn't believe what a whirl-wind the last year and a half had been.

She was grateful for what had happened, to be sure, but there had been such a mad rush of developments that she was still digesting some of them. Charles meeting Annabelle had set into motion a series of events one would hardly expect from a chance encounter in a ballroom.

The Hartleys' trip to Bath had been more serious than a simple season in town—this jaunt had been their last hope. When their father had unexpectedly died, they'd inherited a lot of debt and little money—most of his wealth had been snapped up by General Hartley's group of sycophants through exploitative business practices against a grieving and confused Jasper—and they were at risk of losing their home if they didn't soon come up with the necessary funds to pay for its upkeep. They were hoping to find a wealthy benefactor in Bath from amongst those who had good memories of their father but none bad of Jasper.

Beatrice oftentimes felt sad for her brother. Yes, he was rude. Yes, he was arrogant. Yes, he'd made mistakes in his youth. But he'd been left in a difficult position. His brief period of excessive drinking had led to a lifetime of consequences that would never go away, however much he reformed. The army had been the best experience of his life. He was finally finding purpose to his existence when he'd had to leave it all behind.

She knew he'd hoped that by the time he inherited the family estate, Beatrice would be married, Charles would have a living at his rectory, and Jasper could relinquish the responsibilities that caring for them entailed without leaving his siblings stranded.

For all that he behaved in a cold-hearted, uninterested manner, Jasper really did care about her and Charles. In truth, she was very proud of Jasper. He'd stepped up when he needed to, and more than that, he'd asked for help. For such a proud man as Jasper, to share his strife with another required a Herculean effort. Beatrice was determined to do all she could to help, and so she had shared her brother's burden of seeking charity.

They'd had no joy at all, and then they'd met Annabelle and her uncle. That had been a complete coincidence but had been the luckiest meeting of their life — he knew their father well and had recently come into possession of property located in their home county that he had no idea what to do with. As Mr Daniels had said when he told everyone of his decision, this was the perfect solution to everybody's problems.

That was how Beatrice came to be where she was, safe and warm in a vast castle with nary a problem, when just eighteen months ago, she'd been worrying about whether she'd have enough money for food, let alone a home.

She was aware that this wasn't a long-term solution for the Hartleys, and she knew that the only remaining problem was her spinster status.

It wasn't that she didn't want to get married. She'd always wanted a family of her own, but marriage had simply never happened. As much as she hated to blame Jasper entirely, she knew that his reputation had severely injured her marketability as a potential wife.

There had been a few little romances in her life, but none had ever resulted in anything serious, and she feared that marrying for connection was out of the question, much less marrying for love. It wouldn't be long before she entered her thirtieth year. In English society, it was almost unheard of for a woman past thirty to be proposed to for the first time.

Finding a husband was something she would have to deal with sooner rather than later, or she would have to find a way to support herself as a spinster. She didn't have many talents per se, or at least *feminine* talents that were appropriate for a woman to earn a living from. She couldn't draw, she couldn't design tables or sew particularly well, and she feared she wasn't intelligent enough to be a governess or tutor.

Her strength lay in running an estate. She'd always been interested in how to maintain a proper home, and she'd consistently maintained a strong relationship with the household staff wherever she lived. Her skills were skewed towards finances, organisation, and tenant relations, but society considered the idea of a lady as the head of an estate to be terribly improper, unless she were widowed and rich, as well as possessed of a dominating character and demonstrable ability.

So although she had more to do with the day-to-day running of Godshollow than Jasper did, she would never be legally recognised as the estate manager. That was terribly unfair, but a hard thing to argue, especially as she didn't have a lot of money.

Her best option at the moment was to find a husband who could support her without being completely loathsome company. She hoped the fresh social circle at and around

Godshollow would provide her with a few *options.*

Which was why it was important she finish her letter to Mrs Lutton.

This library was one of her favourite places to be; it was so warm and comfortable. She liked it so much, she'd had her writing desk brought in there.

A flash of lightning illuminated the room and drew her attention back to the writing desk and the writing she'd been doing. When the storm had started, she was halfway through a reply to Mrs Lutton, but the climactic theatrics had diverted her attention. She must finish the letter so it would arrive on time.

She picked up her quill and found where she'd left off.

A masquerade theme for the ball would be a splendid idea.

The ball would give her a chance to find out who among the local gentlemen had a fun spirit, and she could find out about them without betraying her identity or her desperation.

We can discuss the decorations if you would like to come to lunch tomorrow. Unfortunately, I fear that Annabelle will not be of strong enough health to attend a party of any sort. Even though her expected date is before that which you have selected for the ball, whether she has given birth or not by that time, she is not going to be ready for social events.

The news was expected to arrive any time soon, as they were approaching Annabelle's eighth month of pregnancy according to the doctor's calculations. There was a trail of excitement from Godshollow to Oxford about the arrival of the new baby. Even Jasper had seemed interested — if asking whether the whole thing was done with from behind his newspaper at breakfast counted as caring.

Beatrice was so very happy for the parents-to-be. She'd never seen her brother so happy, and Annabelle was as lovely a sister-in-law as she could have ever hoped for. Their marriage was still viewed as quite the miracle given the events that occurred with Mr Evans. The kidnapping had changed them both, for good and for bad. Most importantly, the couple lived every day knowing they were blessed with their lives the way they were.

At this point in time, things seemed to be going very well for everyone. Beatrice vowed to herself she would relax and try to enjoy whatever was happening in the moment, such as it was, and ignore the malicious part of her mind that always wanted to point out fragility and the changeable nature of life.

She was just signing off her last letter when there was a knock at the front door. The sound was almost concealed by a loud crash of thunder, but Beatrice was able to distinguish between the two booms.

She left the library and headed towards the entrance hall, wondering what the odds were of a servant coming to deliver the news of the birth just at the time she'd been thinking about it? Picking up speed, she rushed down the hallway, hoping she'd finally become an aunt, but it was an altogether different visitor who was waiting downstairs.

The newcomer was a man. Definitely a gentleman, he stood proud and tall—and he was *incredibly* tall—as if he was a man who was well aware of his status. His long black hair was tied neatly in a queue by a contrasting light blue ribbon, and whilst his muscular figure suggested he wasn't a stranger to manual labour, his pale complexion asserted the indoor life of a gentleman.

Definitely not a messenger.

He wasn't local. Godshollow was in an area that was lacking in neighbours, which made it very easy to know everyone who lived within a twenty-mile radius. And this man was *not* one of those people.

At first glance, she couldn't really tell where he was from. Whilst his features were strikingly handsome, they were of a generic sort of look that could place him as being from anywhere in England.

Nobody seemed to be attending him, so she decided to greet him. Walking towards him with purpose, she wasn't able to get a word out before he spoke first.

"Finally," he called in a thick Scottish brogue—*definitely not English then*—"I was wondering how long ye were going tae stand there gaping." He clearly thought she was a maid.

This was going to be an interesting conversation.

Chapter Two

Duncan Mackenzie was cold. Cold and wet. Cold and wet *and* tired. And to top it all off, he was waiting to see if his journey of over five hundred miles had all been for naught. All the wind, rain, saddle-soreness, and rein-grip blisters he'd endured could all be for naught in a matter of seconds if he couldn't find the man he was looking for.

A young man had let him in, saying he needed to fetch his master, after informing him that the man Duncan wanted to speak with, Mr Daniels, wasn't there. He'd left Duncan standing in the entrance with little to do other than twiddle his thumbs and drip rainwater onto the perfectly polished floorboards.

Duncan was on edge. His nerves were made worse when he saw a maid deliberately ignore him. She'd come marching down the corridor and had absolutely seen him, only to stand there, a dumb look on her face as she watched him.

With every minute she left him waiting, he grew more and more irate. By the time she did approach, Duncan was in no mood to be forgiving of her behaviour.

"Finally," he cried when she stepped into view. She tried to say something, but he cut her off.

"I know ye saw me."

She looked at him quizzically. "Good evening, my name is —"

Duncan laughed in disbelief. "Look, lass, I dunnae care what yer name is. Tisnae important right now. Just go an' get me a towel. I'm sure yer master wouldnae like me dripping all over yer floors."

A sizable puddle had begun to form around his boots. He gestured towards it to illustrate his point. But *still* the lazy wench tried to talk back.

"If you'll just—"

"Lord help me." Duncan sighed in frustration. "Are all English women this obstinate? If ye willnae help me, at least go and find someone who will."

She nodded and turned on her heel without another word, marching out of the entrance hall. Duncan had no idea if she was actually going to find another servant, or if she'd just decided to leave him to fend for himself.

He began to tap his foot impatiently, sending yet more raindrops to join their brethren in the puddle.

While he was waiting, he took the opportunity to properly survey the room he was standing in. He'd heard so many stories about this place, ever since he was a wee babe-in-arms, and he'd dreamed for so long about finally being here. Now that those dreams were on the cusp of being realised, it wasn't at all what he'd been expecting. The castle was just as grand and exquisite as he'd been led to believe, but it was devoid of the thing he wanted the most—a sense of familiarity. He'd realised this would probably be the case, but it stung no less for his having been prepared for the eventuality.

He had no idea how long he'd been standing there, trying to envision his ancestors, but eventually the first young man came back, followed by another who was clearly the head of the house.

This was a lean man with a lithe presence. His way of walking and holding himself indicated a military career of some sort. Surprisingly, when he reached Duncan, he beamed at him, taking his hand and shaking it vigorously.

"You are Mr Mackenzie, yes?"

"Aye, but—"

"Wonderful." He let go of Duncan's hand and gestured for the Scotsman to follow him. "Regretfully, Mr Daniels is not here at the moment, but he's given me authority to deal with matters in his absence."

He must be a son or nephew of some kind who's running the place fer Daniels.

Duncan tried to keep up with the striding man and found speaking difficult at such a pace. "I dunnae think this is something *ye* can help with."

The gentleman stopped in front of a door. He opened it and ushered Duncan into the room.

"I can assure you, Mr Daniels has every faith in my abilities," he said as he moved to his desk. "I'm sure I can solve whatever little problem you have."

He indicated a seat on the nearest side of the desk for Duncan to sit in.

Duncan sat down and leant back, placing a hand on his chin, trying to phrase his argument. As it was, he was having trouble making sense of this man, who hadn't even given his name and yet seemed far too happy for someone who'd received an unexpected late-night guest.

"I'm sure Mr Daniels values ye very highly, but ma problem isnae one that ye can solve in his stead. Even if you are family."

The man laughed. "I'm not related to Mr Daniels."

"Then who are ye?"

"I'm Major Jasper Hartley. I'm Mr Daniels's tenant. I run Godshollow."

"Well, thank ye fer seeing me, but I really need tae talk tae Daniels instead."

Hartley shook his head. "Look, I'm in charge here. Mr Daniels doesn't like to be disturbed unless the matter is urgent. So you can tell me what's about, and if I can't sort it for you, then I will send for him."

Duncan didn't like having to divulge his plans to more

people than necessary, but he was desperate. And if this was the only way to assure Daniels would see him, then it had to be done.

"Ach! Fine, if it's the only way. I have all the documents in ma bag." He reached down for the sack he'd placed on the floor next to him. As he lifted it, a stream of water flowed down onto the floor. "'Tis rather wet outside," he said sheepishly in answer to Hartley's unimpressed face.

The bag was incredibly wet. Duncan had to hope it had done its job and kept its contents dry. He flipped it open and held his breath.

There had been some leakage, but it looked as though all the important things were dry. He'd specifically placed the papers in the middle so should there be a leak, other material would soak up the water before it could cause damage. He withdrew the bundle and laid it out in front of Hartley, whose eyes went wide when he saw the mass of papers.

"I see," he said cautiously. "Well, I don't really think I'll be able to go through all of this tonight. How about you give me a summary, and I'll look this over in the morning."

Again, Duncan was concerned, but decided to concede the fight to win the war. One thing did concern him. "What am I tae do until then? Where shall I go?"

Hartley's reply surprised him.

"Oh, of course, you must stay here."

"I dunnae think ye'll want me tae, when I explain ma reasons fer being here."

Hartley waved a dismissive hand. "That won't be a problem. So, please, briefly, why are you here?"

Duncan took a deep breath and braced himself.

"I am here as a descendant of Fraser Mackenzie. I've come tae reclaim Godshollow fer the clan Mackenzie."

CHAPTER THREE

Duncan's admission didn't get quite the reaction he was expecting. Major Hartley seemed completely undaunted. He nodded and clicked his tongue, his face expressionless.

"I see," he said again. "That is quite something, isn't it?"

The Major's reaction was disquieting, to say the least. Duncan now had energy built up that he didn't need. He'd been expecting some shouting at least, maybe even a bit of a fight, but this was reasonable and measured.

"In that case, it's definitely better that we defer this until tomorrow. I don't want to miss anything because I'm too tired." Hartley stood and tapped the papers on the table, arranging them in a neat pile. Then he came around the front of his desk to stand next to Duncan. "As I said, you're welcome to stay here, though in light of the current circumstances, I would rather you didn't talk to anyone else about your reasons for being here."

Duncan was still recovering from the shock of such an anticlimactic response. "Aye, I will stay, thank ye." He felt as though his mouth was answering for him whilst his mind was busy figuring out what the hell had just happened. Then something clicked. "I'll agree nae tae say a word, but what do ye want me tae tell anyone that asks?"

"Anything you like," Hartley responded flippantly. "Tell them you're from the circus, for all I care. Just don't tell them about the claim."

Duncan didn't respond verbally, letting a nod suffice.

"Good," Hartley replied curtly. "Now I'll call a servant and we'll get you a room."

Hartley's hospitality was still completely bewildering to Duncan. It wasn't until he was alone in his small, quiet room that he could begin to digest everything that had happened in the last hour or so.

The more he thought about it, the more Hartley's behaviour didn't make sense. Duncan had come into this man's home and told him he wanted to take it from him. There should have been confrontation, not acceptance. Hell, he would have taken a duel right now over this odd behaviour. That was unnerving.

Maybe he wasn't so shocked because it wasn't his property, because he was just a tenant. But that would still be disruptive for him, because Duncan wasn't planning on keeping him around when his claim went through. So why was he so relaxed? He'd seemed almost happy when he greeted him, as though he was expecting him. But how could he expect him? Duncan had made sure nobody knew where he was going. He'd left in the middle of the night to make sure no one followed him.

Between Hartley's odd behaviour and his lacklustre maid, Duncan was sure that staying at Godshollow was going to be an interesting experience.

But he'd made it. Half the battle was over. "I'm here, nanna," he whispered gently as he climbed into bed. He looked around the room and revelled in the accomplishment. "It's going to be all right."

The next morning, Duncan was awakened by a knock on the door.

"Mr Mackenzie, sir. Major Hartley would like to know if you'll be joining him for breakfast."

The loud grumbling of Duncan's stomach made up his mind. "Aye," he called back. "I just need tae get dressed.

Where's the Major?"

The man began to give directions to the breakfast room, but Duncan had as much chance of remembering it all as he did of being struck by lightning. He tried to commit the words to memory, going through the instructions as he dressed, but as soon as he was in the hallway, anything to do with navigation left his mind.

In the end, he started to follow the hallways, choosing randomly, feeling rather like Theseus, wishing he had Ariadne's ball of string. It didn't help that all of the walls seemed to be the same colours.

"'Tis true, the English really have nae sense of style," he muttered to himself as he passed what he thought was the same brown chair for at least the third time. Nevertheless, he continued his quest for breakfast.

As he rounded a corner on the second floor—one floor down from where he'd started, but one up from the first place he'd tried—he saw the maid from the night before. She was happily chatting to another maid whilst neither did any work. They must have heard him coming, because they both looked up. The second maid disappeared down the hall very quickly, but the first had the audacity to greet him with a wide smile.

"Good morning," she said cheerily. "Can I help you with anything?"

"Yer in a better mood this morning," he commented.

"I'm sorry, what?"

Duncan was going to elaborate on her disgraceful manner and woeful work ethic the night before when he saw another man coming down the hallway. He was dressed very smartly, and if he had to guess, Duncan would have identified him as the steward or something of that ilk.

There we are. He'll sort out this wee hellion and give her a proper talking tae.

But that wasn't what happened.

The man went up to the woman, and she greeted him as

cheerily as she'd greeted Duncan.

"Good morning, Mr Peters. How is everything after the storm last night?"

"Quite well, thank you, ma'am. There was a little damage when a felled tree hit the roof of the log store, but the firewood we gained far outweighs any that was lost."

Ma'am?

Ach!

Whatever the expression on his face, Duncan knew she'd seen what he was thinking.

She stepped forwards and held out her hand. "I don't think we've been properly introduced," she said sweetly. "I'm Beatrice Hartley."

Chapter Four

Beatrice knew the exact moment the guest realised she wasn't a servant. His whole expression dropped, as though a puppeteer had cut the strings to his face. She had to try hard not to laugh aloud.

He was absolutely mortified. His shoulders curled forwards, his eyes cast down, and he resembled a child who'd been caught breaking the rules. If she didn't find it so deliciously satisfying to see him realise his mistake, she might have felt sorry for him.

Her hand was still extended towards him, hanging in the air between them. The man looked at it as though she was offering him a live eel. He gingerly put his own hand out and took hers. The shake was practically non-existent.

"Aye. Ah, I'm . . ." He looked as if he was having to think about what to say. Eventually he settled with, "Sorry."

Beatrice smiled brightly at him. "Sorry? Is that your surname or your Christian name?"

His eyes widened and he coughed self-consciously. "That isnae . . . ma name . . . . Ma name is Duncan Mackenzie."

"Pleased to meet you," Beatrice replied, with as broad a grin as she could muster. The way she saw it, the politer she was to him, the guiltier he would feel about being such a lout. Of course, she'd already forgiven him, but he didn't have to know that.

"I assume you're making your way to breakfast?"

Mr Mackenzie nodded.

"Well then, you're in *completely* the wrong end of the castle

20

for that. Luckily, that's also where I'm heading. Follow me."

She started down the corridor and heard Mr Mackenzie's boots hit the floor with a heavy thud each time he took a step.

She wound her way through the hallways, barely using her markers to navigate.

The first time she'd tried to explore the castle she'd gotten completely lost. So in places where it was too small to notice — unless you knew to look for it — she'd taken the chalk from her sewing kit and marked the walls with a number and a letter, one being the floor she was on, the other which wing she was in. The markers helped her to always know where she was in relation to anything, and also told her if she'd just doubled back on herself.

It seemed that Mr Mackenzie was having just as much trouble as she'd once had, as she heard him mutter something about *damned English* and *a bloody labyrinth*. She chuckled to herself.

But what happened next left her completely astonished.

She came to the door of the breakfast room, which was slightly ajar. She pushed on it and motioned for Mr Mackenzie to go through first. As he did so, Beatrice heard her brother speak.

"Good morning, Mr Mackenzie. Did you sleep well?"

That was the weirdest thing she'd ever heard. Jasper was practically being friendly, bordering on enthusiastic. Like seeing a woman wearing britches — it happened occasionally, but so seldom that it appeared odd when it did occur.

When she followed Mr Mackenzie into the room, Jasper didn't say a word to her. To make a point, she parroted his own words to Mackenzie back at him.

He briefly looked at her from over the top of his broadsheet. "Hmm? Yes, quite." Then he turned to Mackenzie. "Come and see me in my study at midday. I should have everything sorted by then."

Sorted? What on earth was he talking about? Clearly, he didn't want her to know what it was they were doing, so why bring it up? This was probably one of his *I'm a man and get to do things, you're a woman and you can't* petty, sly mentions. She wouldn't put it past him. He was *pretty* annoyed that Mr Peters seemed to prefer her to him and openly discussed the housekeeping with her.

Or . . .

Or he wanted her to know that something was wrong without having to shame himself by telling her. That was a pattern with them. Even if Jasper could admit his troubles to Mr Daniels, he couldn't with his own sister. So, knowing she was smart enough to figure it out by herself, he would drop hints so he didn't have to admit he'd done something wrong. Usually, it was . . .

Oh dear. She would have to try and have a private word with Mr Mackenzie later.

Though now was just as good, because Jasper finished his toast and promptly left.

No time like the present.

At first, she just continued to eat her breakfast, not wanting to scare Mr Mackenzie away too quickly. After about five minutes of silent eating from both of them, she tried to break the ice.

"So, your accent," she asked as innocently as she could. "You're from Scotland, yes?"

"Aye," Mr Mackenzie replied warily before turning his attention back to his food. She thought he was still a bit ashamed about thinking her a maid. He wouldn't look her in the eye.

But Beatrice was renowned for her perseverance. "Which part of Scotland? I know my brother spent some time there when he was in the army."

He looked up again but could only make eye contact with

the space just below her left ear. "I dunnae think ye'd of heard of where I'm from."

This was getting her nowhere. She was just going to have to be blunt. "How much does he owe you?" she asked curtly.

Finally, Mackenzie met her eyes. "What are ye talking about, lass?"

"I'm very well aware my brother has outstanding debts. I want to know how much you're due."

"I dunnae know what yer talking about."

"Then why are you here?"

He shook his head. "Yer a forward young lass, aren't ye? But even if ye werenae, I cannae tell ye what I'm doing here."

"Why not?"

"It's private."

"How private?"

"*Very* private."

"But I want to know."

Mr Mackenzie sighed and stroked his chin. "Fine," he said. "But ye cannae tell yer brother I told ye, understand?"

Beatrice leant forwards expectantly. "I promise."

Mackenzie considered for a moment. "I'm from the circus."

That wasn't the answer she'd been expecting. To be honest, Mackenzie didn't sound that sure of his reply himself. She decided to play along.

"Is there a circus in town? Are you here to see it, or perform in it? I do love the circus. I enjoy watching the *jesters*. Indeed, my new sister would love that sort of thing as well, and she does need cheering at the moment."

Beatrice was curious as to how far the man intended to keep up the charade, and whether he would notice her deliberate mistake.

"Aye . . .well . . .it isnae a big thing, ye see. It's fer a select few."

"I see," Beatrice whispered conspiratorially. "Is *that* why you're here? Were you delivering an invitation to my brother?" She was like a prompter giving cues.

"Aye," he replied.

"And what do you do in the circus?"

"I . . . I'm . . .'tis the . . ."

Beatrice watched him fish for words. Five minutes seemed to have gone past by the time he answered.

"I work with the horses."

"Oh. Well, I do beg your pardon," she replied. "Is it only the one horse you brought with you, or are there more?"

"Just the one."

"That will be quite the relief to our stable boy." Mr Mackenzie looked a little sheepish, as well he might. Beatrice had heard the whole tale from Lawrence that morning, how he was less than impressed with being woken in practically the middle of the night to tend to an uninvited stranger's horse.

Mr Mackenzie rose to his feet. "I must go and thank him."

Beatrice smiled. "Of course," she responded. "That would be the proper thing to do."

"Aye." He gave her a small bow and left.

That left Beatrice on her own in the breakfast room to ponder over their new visitor.

It was obvious he wasn't from the circus, but neither did it seem he was collecting a debt from Jasper. Yet the two men were conducting some kind of business, of that she was sure.

But what kind of business? Not many men would insist upon performing any kind of work at such a late hour as their guest had arrived at the night before, so it must be an urgent matter.

The fact that Jasper had allowed the man to stay, coupled with the midday meeting scheduled, meant that this wasn't something that was easily resolved.

Mackenzie wasn't a name that she remembered directly, but something was nagging at her from the back of her mind, as if she *should* know the name.

She needed to find out more about their visitor.

Before Mrs Lutton arrived, she had some research to do.

CHAPTER FIVE

In the three hours between breakfast and Mrs Lutton's arrival, Beatrice was very annoyed that she'd uncovered exactly nothing about their visitor. First, she'd gone to Mr Peters. Being the steward, he could always be relied upon for information about what happened under their roof, and his years of service in the area had given him good knowledge of the surrounding neighbourhoods. Unfortunately, he hadn't been able to give her any information—he knew as little about the stranger as she did.

"You're right though," he commented thoughtfully. "Something tells me I should be familiar with the name. It's just not one I've come across in town."

Next she spoke to Tobias and learnt he'd been the one to let Mr Mackenzie in the night before and reported his arrival to Jasper, but he wasn't much help either.

"I'm sorry, Miss Beatrice. I couldn't really understand what he was saying, his accent was so very thick and he was so cross. I thought it would be best to get Major Hartley right away."

"You did well," she assured him. "But you're certain he didn't say anything about why he was here?"

"No, Miss. Though I think he wanted Mr Daniels rather than the Major. That's what he was cross about, I think."

"Really?"

"Yes, Miss."

That was interesting. Mr Mackenzie's visit wasn't intended for Jasper, and that bit of information changed things. Because

Mr Daniels had left the day-to-day running of Godshollow to Jasper, it was very rare that anyone came to them actually looking for the owner, since he was far away in Oxfordshire.

Any problems with the estate could normally be handled by Jasper. If Mr Mackenzie was looking for Mr Daniels instead, odds were that the issue was outside of the normal topics discussed in Jasper's study.

Armed with this new knowledge, she redoubled her efforts, inquiring from the remaining staff—the cook, her maid, and the stableboy—if they knew anything that Tobias or Mr Peters didn't, but nobody had a single piece of information.

It was clear that Mr Mackenzie wasn't involved with anyone on the estate and wasn't from any of the businesses Godshollow dealt with in the town. His connections didn't pertain to anything in Godshollow's present.

So, perhaps, Mr Mackenzie's ties—and hopefully his reasons for being there—lay in Godshollow's past.

Beatrice knew that the Gordon family had lived here before them, the late Mr Gordon being the one who gifted it to Mr Daniels. Mr Daniels had inherited the current staff from the Gordons as well as the castle—this was their home, and Mr Daniels was happy to keep them on—and if they couldn't remember the name Mackenzie, odds were he had nothing to do with the Gordons' tenure either. Another dead end.

Then Beatrice remembered the story Jasper had told Annabelle when they'd dined together for the first time. He had marvelled at Annabelle's lack of knowledge, but delighted in telling the story of the family who had built Godshollow, only to sadly become victims of the Civil War. Maybe she would find reference to the Mackenzie family somewhere in that family's time at the castle.

The best place to look would be the castle records held in the library. Beatrice had discovered their existence during an exploration one day, curious to find out what reading material was available at Godshollow.

She had intended to explore the library but was prevented by Mrs Lutton's arrival.

Mrs Lutton—and her husband when he accompanied her—were the most frequent visitors to Godshollow. The sixty-year-old woman had become one of Beatrice's best friends. To be honest, after everything they'd all been through with Annabelle and her ordeal with Gregory Evans, there was no way they all weren't going to become closer.

Well, all of them except for Jasper. Jasper wasn't close to anyone. He had respect for a few people, army acquaintances mostly, but it was impossible to say if he actually liked anyone. This made his jovial reception of Mr Mackenzie very peculiar indeed.

Whether Jasper liked her or not, Mrs Lutton was a very good friend to Beatrice, quite possibly the closest she'd had to a mother figure.

When Beatrice met her in the parlour, Mrs Lutton greeted Beatrice with a warm hug. "How are you, my dear? Thank you for inviting me. Has Annabelle begun her lying-in yet?"

Beatrice greeted her with open arms and a big smile. "Not yet, though it should be any day now."

"Well, I'm very excited to meet baby Angela."

Beatrice laughed. "What if it's a boy?"

"Angelo?"

Beatrice laughed at the joke, but even to her own ears it wasn't whole-hearted. She just couldn't stop thinking about what Mr Mackenzie was doing. Mrs Lutton fixed her with one of her shrewd looks.

"What aren't you telling me? Is there a complication with the pregnancy?"

"No, no. Not at all." Beatrice paused before continuing, trying to figure out where to start. Eventually she told Mrs Lutton about their visitor, starting with, "I don't suppose you've been invited to the circus, have you?"

Mrs Lutton hadn't been invited to the circus. She hadn't even heard of one's coming to town in the upcoming months.

"Very peculiar. You suppose he isn't telling the truth?" she speculated.

"I'm *certain* he's not telling the truth," Beatrice replied. "I wanted to see if this was a ruse he put effort into or something he just blurted out to me when I questioned him. I suppose if I was ever going to use a thing like a circus to cover up my true intentions I would make as much a commotion about it as I could, only for it to be conveniently called off *at the last minute* owing to a tragic accident or some such."

Mrs Lutton laughed. "I fear, my dear, there are few who share your quick imagination. That being said, I will keep an eye out on your behalf."

That ended the conversation for a little while as the ladies drank some tea.

"It's all very exciting," Mrs Lutton remarked at length. "A mysterious visitor with an unconvincing story." Then she laughed. "Listen to me, I sound like one of the market gossips."

"And just what are you suggesting?" Beatrice retorted with a smile.

"Nothing, indeed. I mean no insult per se. That was more a detrimental remark on my age. I'm far too old to be getting involved with anything that smacks of intrigue or mystery."

"From what Annabelle told me of her ordeal, I would say you've never been a lady to idly watch action pass her by."

Mrs Lutton's lips curled into a small smile, deepening the laughter lines on her cheeks. "That wasn't anything spectacular," she countered. "That was just what needed doing."

The ladies fell back into a comfortable silence, each pondering the situation.

"You say the man's name is Mackenzie?"

Beatrice nodded.

"Perhaps George might know something. He's lived in this area far longer than I have, and he's very good at remembering names."

"If you wouldn't mind asking him?"

"I don't mind at all. Now, let us get to the important business. Is it too late to change the decorations for the ball to Scottish?"

It was well into the evening by the time Mrs Lutton left. Beatrice could tell she wanted to stay for dinner and meet their mysterious gentleman, but General Lutton had physically come to retrieve her for a night out at the theatre.

Left alone, Beatrice's thoughts fell back to the mysterious Mr Mackenzie. She decided she needed to speak to her brother and find out what was really going on. She went to the ground floor study where she knew he would be. There were three studies in the castle, one each on the ground, first and second floors. Two were presumably for the use of any guests, whilst one was for the master. Jasper had chosen the one with the most space for himself.

When she arrived at the room, Beatrice didn't even knock but simply went straight in, determined she wasn't going to let him fob her off.

"Do come in by all means," Jasper said sarcastically although she already stood opposite him.

"*What* is going on?" she demanded.

Jasper's features relaxed. "Going on?" he echoed. His feigning ignorance just made Beatrice more infuriated.

"That's enough, Jasper," she said shortly. "You know why Mr Mackenzie is here, and I deserve to know as well."

Jasper smiled at her smugly. "It's nothing you need worry yourself with," he replied patronisingly.

"Nothing . . . argh." Beatrice threw her hands in the air.

"Stop treating me like I'm a child. I know that he's really here to see Mr Daniels. That means he's here about something big. And if this *is* big, it *does* concern me, and I *will* worry about it. I live here too."

"We are *not* talking about this," he said firmly.

"Yes, we are," Beatrice replied. She put her hands on her hips and tried to stare him down.

"*No*," Jasper asserted. "*I'm* the head of this house and you will do what I say."

"But it's not even your house, is it? Does Mr Daniels even know about our *guest*?"

That caught Jasper's attention. His answer was rushed and had an air of panic about it.

"Of course I've made Mr Daniels aware we have a visitor. But as it is, there's nothing of immediate concern that he needs to be informed about. Rest assured if anything escalates, I will notify him immediately."

"What's going to *escalate*?" She was *not* going to back down.

Jasper sighed. "Nothing is going to escalate. I said *if*. Look, just leave it with me for now. I *suggest* you give Mr Mackenzie a wide berth." His tone made clear his suggestion was actually an order. "You have more important things to be doing. Preparing for tonight, for example."

"Tonight?" She was getting sick of having to ask all these questions.

"Yes. Mr Ocheridge is coming for dinner. I informed you of the engagement a week ago."

She'd forgotten all about that. What with the excitement of a mysterious visitor, the lawyer from the town had slipped her mind. She wasn't fond of seeing Mr Ocheridge, finding him to be arrogant and impersonable. To her dismay, her brother had been dropping various hints that Ocheridge would make her a good husband. Beatrice was clearly fast running out of matrimonial options, but she wouldn't go down without a fight.

"Is it wise to have him here along with our new visitor? Surely, it would be best to wait until things with Mr Mackenzie are resolved. You clearly don't want even *me* to know what's going on here. We can't keep introducing new people into this odd situation. Perhaps we should send a note and ask him to come back another day?"

Jasper's response was a great deal more forceful than she expected.

"No," he barked harshly. "Don't be so ridiculous. Ocheridge is an honoured guest. I would never turn him away, even if the king himself was dining with us. Now leave me alone and go and get dressed. He'll be arriving at seven o'clock."

There was no more arguing to be done, and Beatrice didn't want to spend the evening going round in circles with her obstinate brother, so she let the matter rest and left the study.

If Ocheridge was coming at seven, that gave her two hours, most of which would be taken up with getting dressed for the evening. Jasper was very insistent on formalwear for dinner, especially if they had company. So for Beatrice, preparing to eat dinner with her brother and his friend was tantamount to getting ready to attend a ball.

She was of two minds about getting dressed up. She didn't like the length of time required to get ready—all the hours spent curling her hair, the layers upon layers of clothes she would have to don. But there was something she liked about looking her very best that gave her a different kind of confidence. She did look good when she was in her finery. But she had to be in the mood for it, and that day she wasn't.

She tried to be chatty and friendly with Matilda, the maid who came to help her dress, but she felt more like a doll being played with than a person—an apt description of how she felt in her life in general, thanks to Jasper's treatment of her. As

Matilda was tightening the corset strings, it occurred to Beatrice to check whether Mr Mackenzie had been informed about dinner. She wasn't sure about Scottish rules regarding guests and formalwear, so she asked Matilda to send Toby to advise him about following Jasper's demands.

CHAPTER SIX

Brushing Bucephalus's hair was something that always calmed Duncan, and he certainly needed calming at that moment. Nobody was supposed to be here. A retired naval officer was supposed to be running Godshollow, not a stuck-up young man and his strong-willed, smart, sharp, witty, charming sister.

What on earth had he been thinking when he told her he was from the circus? It was definitely one of the stupidest things he'd said in his life. He knew she knew it was a lie. A person would have to be incredibly gullible to believe him. And yet he'd continued, taking the deception further with each new detail.

Regardless of Hartley saying neither of them could mention the matter at hand, Duncan knew Miss Hartley would figure out the truth eventually. The question was, was it better for her to find out for herself, or for him to tell her?

At midday, just as requested, Duncan went to visit Major Hartley in his study. He'd hoped he would remember the way from the night before, but he was found by a servant two floors up and three corridors in the wrong direction from where he should have been.

Therefore, it was actually a little after twelve o'clock before he was able to see Hartley. From what the young servant said, Major Hartley was not one who liked to be kept waiting. He fully expected a cool reception to his late arrival, but Hartley didn't even mention it. He welcomed Duncan into the room and offered him a seat. He had an odd energy about him that put Duncan on his guard.

"Thank you for coming," the Englishman said with a smile. "I've reviewed your papers and I've written to Mr Daniels on the matter." Duncan was about to thank him gratefully, but Hartley held up a hand and stopped him. "However, in all probability, it will be upwards of a month before we see him. He is a very busy man, and Oxfordshire is a long ride from here."

That seemed reasonable. It had to be, as Duncan didn't have another choice. "Thank ye," he replied. "How far is it tae the nearest inn? I'll need tae book a room fer a long time it seems."

Once again, Hartley surprised him. "Don't be ridiculous. You will stay here."

"Is that really wise?" Duncan asked in astonishment. "I cannae help but feel that ye arenae taking this seriously. Ye understand what it is I'm here tae do, and what that could mean fer ye and yer sister?"

"Of course I do," Hartley answered hurriedly. "I just thought it might save you some money."

That wasn't a strong argument, and Hartley's tone made Duncan uneasy. He sounded almost desperate, an emotion Duncan could justify in the situation, but his desperation was for all the wrong reasons. He *should* have been desperate to keep Duncan from arguing the ownership, not be anxious to keep a potential home-taker from staying in said home.

Residing at Godshollow *would* be the best option for Duncan. Indeed, it was what he'd intended to do in the first place. But that was when he'd thought Godshollow was only inhabited by a lonely old man. Now he feared that spending too much time with Major—and particularly Miss—Hartley might cause him difficulties. Despite the way his uncle had raised him, Duncan wasn't heartless, and the thought of having to make such a nice young lass as Miss Hartley homeless was gnawing away at his resolve.

However, whatever bad situation he would inflict upon the Hartleys, it couldn't be as bad as his own distressing circumstances. He *needed* Godshollow. If he couldn't have it, he had nothing left. After everything he'd been through, he had to put himself first, however uncomfortable that made him feel.

Duncan and Hartley had gone back and forth for nearly an hour, debating whether he should stay at Godshollow, but eventually Duncan relented. As much as he feared complications from remaining in the household, he couldn't give up the chance to explore Godshollow properly. He wanted to bask in the memory of his ancestors.

He'd grown up on stories of Godshollow. His father, before he died, and later his grandmother—another who'd been taken from him—loved to tell the tale of brave Laird Fraser, especially the heroic last stand of Godshollow.

It was for them that he was here now. His great-grandparents had applied for ownership a long time ago, before Duncan was even born. They were the remaining heirs of Fraser Mackenzie, the Scotsman who became an English lord. As his descendants, they believed Godshollow belonged to them, but they didn't have the money to fight a lengthy court battle to prove that Cromwell's confiscation of it was no longer valid because of the Restoration of the Monarchy.

The family had always kept an ear out for news of Godshollow, using their local lawyer to keep themselves informed. Though they'd never used the lawyer professionally, he pitied their circumstances, and while he couldn't work for free, he could help keep news of Godshollow flowing to Scotland. Their hearts had broken when they received the news that the manor had been given to someone else.

The relationship with the law firm had been passed down

the generations, and that was how Duncan had heard God-shollow had been given to a Brigadier Daniels. He saw this as his opportunity.

After his nanna had died, Duncan knew it was only a matter of time before he was thrown out of his home by an uncle who had never liked him — she'd been the only one who could protect him. But that had proved to be fortuitous timing.

He decided he would claim the castle before Daniels had a chance to settle in and fulfil his nanna's wish to have the Mackenzie line in Godshollow once again. It was just a shame she wasn't around to see that happen.

He remembered her beaming smile as she relayed the stories she'd been told by her own parents, encouraging his adventurous spirit, despite his mother's wishes.

"Duncan, ma boy, what are ye doing?" His mother watched him with curiosity as he set out lines of pinecones on the bar.

"I'm playing war," he replied brightly. *"These are ma men, and we're defending the castle from the English just like Sir Fraser did."* He'd arranged a set of tankards between the cones to serve as the castle wall.

This did not impress his mother. She sighed deeply and put her hands on her hips, her foot tapping against the floor. *"Has yer nanna been telling stories again?"* She looked shrewishly at his elderly nanna, who sat in the corner. His nanna was always tasked with looking after him when the inn got busy. *"I've told ye nae tae talk about it, Cait,"* she said angrily. Then she turned to Duncan. *"And I told ye nae tae listen an' all. What did I tell ye?"*

Duncan began collecting the pinecones into his arms. *"Nae tae let nanna tell me stories about Fraser."*

"Aye," his mother replied. *"And what did I say the punishment would be fer that?"*

"Let him be, Judith." His grandmother had finally spoken up. *"There's nae harm in telling the lad some stories. Come here, Mo gràidh."* She held her arms out for Duncan.

"He's ma son," his mother rebutted harshly, *pulling Duncan back by his shirt collar. "I'll nae be having ye filling his head with nonsense. Now off tae bed with ye."*

Despite his mother's warning, his nanna continued to proudly tell him the tales of his ancestors.

Losing his father at the age of five had been hard, but losing his nanna in the last six months had broken him. Especially as he held himself responsible for her death, unable to ease her pain through the horrible illness that had worn her down as he watched helplessly. He missed her every day, and the loss felt far greater here. He hadn't realised how much seeing this place would affect him. He'd hoped that being in the home of his ancestors would fill the familial void left by his nanna, but it seemed to only exacerbate it.

He felt lost, and not just because the castle was a bloody maze. Every day he struggled against the panic that gripped him, working hard to oppose the sense of despair that had plagued him since his formative years.

His uncle had always feared Duncan would grow up to overthrow him as head of the clan, especially as the leadership was Duncan's by right. And so he'd raised the young boy horribly, working to quash any spirit, determination, strength, or self-esteem in the hopes of keeping his nephew under his control.

If it hadn't been for his nanna, Duncan was loathe to think of who he might have become. He was indebted to her, and claiming Godshollow for the clan Mackenzie was his way of repaying her.

The emotional struggles of the day had sent Duncan to sleep before he'd even had any lunch. He'd taken his bag to his room and unpacked the small number of possessions he'd been able to bring, and then flopped on the bed, falling asleep almost immediately.

Most important among the items he'd brought was a miniature of his nanna and his father. The painting was housed in a small frame no taller than his thumb, which made it easy to carry around with him. He set it up on the small vanity that had been placed so the sitter could look out over the grounds as they brushed their hair and washed their face. It felt important to face the miniature towards the view, letting the paintings see what their subjects never would.

He'd brought very little else with him. The papers which he'd given to Hartley to look over had taken up much of the room. In the remaining available space he'd packed two shirts, his kilt, which he wore now he didn't need his riding breeches, hose, sporran, and a coat. That, added to what he was currently wearing, made up his entire wardrobe. A very few personal items, such as the portraits which meant so much to him and the money his nanna had given to him before she died, were the last few things that completed his luggage.

Another part of his uncle's attempts to enfeeble Duncan was making sure he had as few things of his own as possible. Duncan supposed the man's thinking was that if he had to rely on other people for everything, he wouldn't want to challenge them and would stay subservient.

In part, his plan had worked. Making Duncan dependent on him put his uncle in a position of power. However, the plan backfired when Graeme's attempts to undermine his self-confidence made Duncan very wary of being seen as a burden and made him determined to look after himself. Also, his nanna seemed delighted to undermine his uncle at every possible turn and had bestowed upon him a few gifts over the years that were *their little secret.*

Unfortunately, his hasty flight from Scotland meant that most of anything he'd managed to procure for himself over the years had to be left behind. The unpacking hadn't taken more than five minutes, leaving Duncan with little to do except to sleep.

"Mr Mackenzie, sir?"

The insistent knocking that accompanied the call roused Duncan from sleep.

"Mr Mackenzie? Miss Beatrice wanted me to see if you require help dressing for dinner."

Duncan stretched and rolled off the bed. His body clicked and popped as he moved—he'd been riding nonstop for at least the last week.

When he opened the door, he was faced with the young lad—Tommy or Toby or something like that—who had allowed him in the night before.

"I'm perfectly capable of dressing maself, thank ye."

The boy's eyes widened. "Of course, sir. What I meant to say is there's a dress code that Major Hartley likes to enforce for dinner. Miss Beatrice was concerned that it may not have been something you would've expected."

The servant was pale and nervous, his eyes boring holes into the floor, his speech high-pitched and fast. Duncan felt sorry for the poor boy. What kind of master would make his servants so afraid to talk to him?

"I see. That's very kind of ye, lad, I appreciate the warning. Thank yer mistress fer me and let her know I have ma formalwear."

He'd packed his kilt without a second thought. He knew Englishmen still struggled to deal with people so overtly Scottish as to wear a kilt, but he hoped the formality would give him a more serious appearance his host could respect.

The boy gave a short bow and left Duncan to dress alone.

As Duncan began to put on his finest clothes, he wondered about the logic of Major Hartley's rule. No doubt he was merely asking for smart, clean, non-daywear clothes, not the elaborate dress of the Highlands, but Duncan didn't have anything else. As far as he was concerned, such a rule was inane, and maybe his outfit would suggest as such to Major Hartley.

Nevertheless, when he was visited again, by Toby or Tommy, to take him down to the dining room, he was impeccably dressed.

CHAPTER SEVEN

When Mr Mackenzie came down to dinner dressed in his Scottish costume, Beatrice wasn't able to think about anything else. His garb was unlike anything she'd ever seen. The men she knew were all stuffy members of the ton, keen to prove their lineage and intellect—almost afraid of any physical exercise. Even Jasper and Charles leant more in that direction, physically.

This man was different. He was powerfully built—his body made for doing, not for sitting behind a desk shuffling papers—and his kilt and coat showed him to his best advantage.

"Mr Mackenzie, thank you for joining us."

Jasper's greeting brought Beatrice out of her reverie, and she realised she'd been staring. Mackenzie realised it, too, if the smirk on his face was anything to go by.

Beatrice sat down and tried to recover from her embarrassment. Jasper, meanwhile, was introducing Mr Mackenzie to Mr Ocheridge.

"Mr Ocheridge is considered to be the best lawyer in town," Jasper bragged.

"Oh, aye?" Mr Mackenzie replied. "Is that Mr Ocheridge of Widdersham and Ocheridge? I've been speaking with yer man, Tunstable."

Beatrice was listening to the conversation, watching the men interact. Once again, her brother was behaving very oddly. To add to the oddity, Ocheridge seemed brimming with barely concealed excitement as he was introduced to the

Scotsman. Even more peculiar, when Mr Mackenzie mentioned the name Tunstable, she noticed Ocheridge's face flash with panic for a brief moment.

"Yes," the lawyer replied eventually. "Good man, Tunstable."

"I've never heard you mention him," Jasper responded. "I thought it was just you and Widdersham in the building."

"He's new," Ocheridge replied, far too quickly. "He's been treating you well, Tunstable?

"Aye. Now that I'm here, I'll have tae get an appointment and meet him properly. Can ye arrange it fer me?"

Ocheridge fidgeted in his seat. "Yes . . ." he said at length, though he didn't sound completely sure. "I'll speak to him in the morning."

"Thank ye."

That ended the conversation for a short while, and even in the silence, Beatrice found her attention drawn to Mr Mackenzie. He was watching Jasper and Ocheridge, but when she caught his eye, he gave her a small smile.

The smile didn't seem to sit well with Ocheridge.

"Miss Beatrice, can I tell you how ravishing you look this evening?" He gave Mackenzie a satisfied smirk after he delivered his *compliment*. But it wasn't the victory he thought it was. His overzealous choice of vocabulary was a little inappropriate, and Beatrice noticed even Jasper was taken aback, but Ocheridge was too important a connection to Jasper for her to start an argument. She decided that her best option to divert the awkward feeling was humour.

"I'm sure you are a far better judge of your ability to give me a compliment than I am."

She received a glare from Jasper for her troubles, but any chastisement was better than what would no doubt have followed if she'd openly insulted him, especially since Ocheridge didn't seem to realise she was laughing at him. He was still attempting to charm her, as usual.

"You know, Mr Tunstable is certainly a good man," Ocheridge remarked as the soup was brought out. "But I've always said that if you were a man, Miss Hartley, you would have made an excellent lawyer."

Beatrice had to swallow her laughter as Mr Mackenzie choked on his soup, and even Jasper made a face. She couldn't understand how her brother thought this man was a good potential husband.

"Thank you?" she replied, trying hard not to snap at him.

Mr Ocheridge hummed thoughtfully. "It really is a man's world, law. Though you have grasped the basics much quicker than many other of your sex."

There were moments in Beatrice's life when she wished the ground would open up and swallow her. Indeed, it could swallow Mr Ocheridge instead if she didn't have to talk to him.

She quickly moved the conversation on.

"Mrs Lutton has received replies to nearly all of her invitations," she commented cheerily to her brother. "This will be a well-attended event, for certain."

Jasper was in polite company, so he had to say something. "Really?" The one-word response showed the requisite social minimum, with an undertone that he didn't really care about the answer.

"She has settled on masquerade for a theme." A thought struck her. "Though as for decoration, with our new guest, she may want to add a circus flavour to the proceedings." She revelled in the raised eyebrows of the three men that her facetiousness had caused. "She mentioned having seen a circus at the *Amphithéâtre Anglais* when she and General Lutton went to Paris—frankly I think she's upset that she never became an acrobat. The way she talked about them, with all the flipping and tumbling and ropes and ribbons—"

"I certainly hope she isn't planning to let the party spill out to Godshollow as well. A circus? *Here?*" Jasper interjected.

Beatrice turned her most withering look on him. "The event shall be contained at Havenbrooke, of course. Mr Mackenzie, you may be called upon to lend assistance."

Mr Mackenzie smiled awkwardly. "I'd be glad tae be of assistance, lass," he responded with an unsure tone.

Jasper's face morphed into confusion, then some kind of bemused understanding. But as always, Ocheridge had to have the biggest portion of attention. Not to be outdone, he loudly added his tuppence worth. "You know, Miss Hartley, I have *some* experience in the circus world. I represented a bearded woman in a fraud case."

"Did ye win?" Mackenzie asked with a tongue-in-cheek tone.

Ocheridge's eyes shifted. "It wasn't anything *I* did," he assured them. "*Any*one would have thought that was a real beard."

The conversation lulled as more courses were brought out and the four of them filled their stomachs. Every now and again someone would say something, though it usually drew one-word answers, or nods of agreement.

Beatrice used this time to watch Mr Mackenzie. She was studying him, looking for the tiniest hint as to who he really was. He had a very animated face. His smile was full, his frown a beautifully expressive crescent, his eyes bright and spirited. But for all that, Beatrice had trouble reading him.

Usually, she was able to easily tell when someone was using a fake smile or expression to hide their true feelings. Not a lot of people were strong enough to maintain a facade for an extended period of time. But Mr Mackenzie's face gave nothing away. She was quite put out, actually, as she'd always considered herself a good judge of character and a fluent reader of people.

Her attention turned to the two men she knew she could read like a well-thumbed book. They'd moved from the table to the fireplace mantle under a clearly false petition from Ocheridge to have more information about a certain painting. Their true purpose seemed to be a private conversation, though, as they were clearly excited and kept looking to Mr Mackenzie in such a way that made obvious to everyone they were talking about him.

Eventually they broke up their little conclave to acknowledge the others. Jasper stood.

"Beatrice, I will ask you to leave the room, please. I need to speak with Mr Ocheridge in my study."

Beatrice tilted her head, perplexed. "If you're going to your study, why do I have to leave the dining room?"

Jasper pointedly looked to Mr Mackenzie. He really was serious about her not talking to him, wasn't he?

A significant argument hung in the air like a mist, waiting for someone to blow the first ball of hot air, but Beatrice decided that wouldn't do her any good.

This time she would let Jasper win — surrender the battle to win the war. That would give her more time to do some research.

"I wouldn't want to get in the way," she conceded graciously. She rose and offered a small curtsey to Mr Mackenzie, who dipped his head, and she bid her brother and Mr Ocheridge good night.

Instead of going left to her room however, she went the other way, racing to the library. She hoped there would be books about the history of the building and the local area that might hold the answer to Mr Mackenzie's visit.

Her studies took her into the early hours of the morning. She'd gone through tome after tome, until the words started to dance on the page and blur together as the candle burned down, giving no useful light anymore.

Unfortunately, the records only went back as far as the first person to have ownership after the Civil War. She might not know exactly who built Godshollow—even the staff didn't know the name—but the story was well known that the man who built the castle was arrested and had the building taken from him.

There was the deed signed in 1712 giving the empty estate to the Gordon family, and the subsequent paperwork for Mr Daniels. As far as anyone need be concerned, that was all they needed to know about the origins of Godshollow. If Beatrice's relatives hadn't been interested in the property and passed down the story about the original owners out of spite for the Gordons when *they* didn't get the property, it was quite possible that nobody would have given the matter any thought given the conspicuous absence of any papers before the Gordons moved in.

There were a few loose floor plans from the original build, but they only bore the signature of the architect, Jean Luc Balfour, so weren't helpful.

As the property had been unoccupied for over a decade by the point that the first Mr Gordon was given it, there wasn't an original owner to sign over the rights. It was simply listed as formerly belonging to the crown. It seemed that the deal had been legalised by the district magistrate upon consent of the King, and there was nothing to suggest that anyone had disputed the deal, either.

As Beatrice had suspected, there was no mention of a Mackenzie in the modern records, so she was forced to conclude that if there was a Mackenzie in Godshollow's history, they came earlier in the story. She just needed the earlier records.

It seemed though, that nothing of that nature was in the library. That made a certain sort of sense, she supposed, even with a lack of evidence of dispute of ownership at the time. If the only papers that existed were the Gordon family's and Mr

Daniels's, it would be more difficult for the property to be disputed in the future.

There was nothing for her to search to find the name Mackenzie. After hours of poring over books and papers, she had hit the end of her ability. Tired and grumpy, she had to admit defeat and go to bed. In the morning, hopefully, Mrs Lutton might return with information from her husband, and if not, Beatrice would have to rethink what she should do.

As she tiptoed quietly along the corridors to her room, she discovered she wasn't the only one having a midnight wander. As she moved down to the first floor, she saw Mr Mackenzie coming up. He looked tired. From his attire, he'd obviously tried to sleep and left his bed when he couldn't, not bothering to properly dress. He wore a long shirt, untied and untucked, over a simple pair of breeches.

Even with her overworked brain, she could appreciate the embarrassment of the situation, particularly because the sight of him gave her flutterings in her stomach.

"Ye cannae sleep either?" the Scotsman asked quietly.

"Lost track of time," Beatrice informed him.

"What were ye doing?"

"Reading."

"Anything interesting?"

Beatrice smiled gently. "Just the history of Godshollow. I find it all very *interesting*."

Mr Mackenzie grimaced. "Oh, aye?"

Beatrice hummed and rocked back on her heels, hoping her bluff would work. "Yes. I thought the name Mackenzie sounded familiar, so I went to see if I'd seen it in the records. I couldn't find it in any of my novels, so that seemed the natural place to look next."

A fleeting expression of panic crossed over Mackenzie's face, long enough to show Beatrice she was following the right thread in looking at the records.

"Did ye find anything?"

Nothing useful. She was going to have to try and lead him into admitting the facts himself.

"Should I have?"

He paused briefly. She could see him thinking—his nose crinkled and his forehead furrowed.

"What do ye know?"

"Why don't *you* tell me what I *should* know?"

That was a mistake. He relaxed a little.

"Nae." Short and clear. He didn't intend to expand her knowledge at all.

His attitude angered her. She was too tired to care about politeness and decorum. She wanted answers.

"Yes. *You* are in *our* home. *You* need to tell *me* why."

Then he said something that took her by surprise.

"Dunnae start on who owns this house, lass. Ye willnae like the answer."

CHAPTER EIGHT

That was absolutely the stupidest thing Duncan could have said. What on earth had he been thinking?

Oh, that's right. Ye werenae thinking at all!

That feisty woman, so like the Valkyries his grandma had told him stories of, had ambushed him on the stairs. When she began to talk, he feared she'd found out about the claim. She hadn't. But, like an idiot, he'd fought back against her rage and revealed himself in his anger.

Dunnae start on who owns this house, lass.

Good going, Mackenzie. Great job.

However, to the girl's credit, she reacted in the manner he'd expected of Major Hartley.

"What do you mean?" Her voice was low and level, and she wasn't showing any weakness. "Mr Daniels owns Godshollow."

"Aye . . ." Duncan said as plainly as he could.

"You don't sound certain. I've just been looking at the paperwork to prove it."

"I'm sure ye have."

"And what? You think there's something wrong with the paperwork? Are you here to take it from him?"

"It isnae that simple."

"Then explain it to me."

"Nae."

"No?" She was brimming with anger, like a kettle coming to a boil on the stove. He watched colour rise up her face. "Why not?"

"I cannae tell ye."

"Can't, or won't?"

"Listen, lass, it isnae ma decision. Yer brother has asked me nae tae talk about it."

No. That was the stupidest thing he could have said. Miss Hartley looked as though she was going to murder him—and he was sure she could do it. He braced himself for a barrage of insults, accusations, and no doubt some angry fists. Instead, Miss Hartley simply turned on her heel and walked away.

He called after her. "Wait, please! Just listen tae me."

That caught her attention. She spun back around to face him. "No," she hissed. "You listen to me. I've had enough of being treated like this—I'm going to bed. Tomorrow—today—at breakfast, unless you're going to tell me what's going on, I don't want you to talk to me at all. And you can say the same to my good-for-nothing brother when you go and report to him what a nosy little busybody I am."

"Miss Hartley—" He reached for her, but she snatched her hand out of his reach.

"I'm serious, Mr Mackenzie."

The battle was lost. Duncan brought his hand back to his side and let her go.

He was stunned. She was right, of course. He knew only too well what it was like to be left out of the loop, treated like an incompetent child. The next morning, he would tell her everything. That was, *if* she would listen to him.

He'd walked into something very unsettling here at Godshollow, but it would all be worth it in the end.

Before that could happen, he needed to inform Hartley of his sister's knowledge, though he intended to leave his own participation in her realisation to a minimum.

That would have to be at a more reasonable hour. On his wandering, he'd passed the study. Major Hartley had definitely gone to bed. It was for the best, really, because he was sure he needed rest to have enough strength for that conversation.

He tried not to look guilty as he entered the study at around eight o'clock the next morning

"I think we need tae talk," he announced, shutting the door firmly.

"Oh?" Major Hartley's tone was curious but mostly cordial.

"Aye." Duncan paused. Hartley had been nothing but courteous to him since he arrived, but he'd seen enough of the man's behaviour towards Miss Hartley that he knew he wasn't always so, and he was worried about the man's reaction. It was infuriating to go through a third man like this, but the letter to Mr Daniels had been sent, so he just had to make nice until he arrived.

"I think ye need tae talk tae yer sister about what's going on here."

Major Hartley's posture straightened, pushing him up to a full sitting height. When he spoke, there was clear evidence he was having to work at keeping his voice level.

"This has nothing to do with her."

"That isnae how she feels about it."

Duncan watched as Hartley tightened his fist on the desk, his hand going white, no doubt a sign of suppressed rage. "What have you told her?" The accusation was thick.

"I havenae told her anything," he lied. "But she was reading the Godshollow records last night, so she tells me. And now she thinks she knows what's happening and is demanding an explanation." He definitely wasn't going to include the part about his blurted house-ownership blunder.

Hartley sighed tiredly. "Of course she is." He rubbed his hand over the top of his head. "Just ignore her. I've already spoken to her about her place in this. She's just being wilful. If you refuse to give her information, she'll give up eventually."

That didn't sound right to Duncan.

"I dunnae think—"

"Look, I know *my* sister better than *you* do. I don't want her to have to deal with this."

There it was, that tiny hint that Hartley was being more than simply controlling, that he actually cared for his sister. His statement could have been interpreted as he just didn't want to give her any power, but his tone suggested a desire to prevent pain rather than deny agency.

"However," Hartley added ominously. "I'm going to keep hold of your papers until Daniels arrives. She won't be able to find them if they're with me. But if I get the slightest hint you've been talking to Beatrice, they might *accidentally* become lost. Think of it as insurance."

Major Hartley had just lost any goodwill he'd gained. Duncan was furious. "Ye cannae do that!"

"Can't I? The way I see it, I hold all the cards here. I can do whatever I want."

And out came Hartley's true nature. The geniality had been an act. Now Duncan met the shrewd, powerful Hartley who thought the world of himself and thought of others as less than dirt. But he had Duncan trapped. He was right, he held all the cards. Did Duncan dare risk his claim to Godshollow for an inquisitive young woman who would most likely hate him if she found out the truth? He had very few options left if he couldn't secure Godshollow. The small inheritance his nanna had given him would carry him for a while, but he dreaded to think of being stranded in England looking for a house or a job. He needed to keep his case alive. From what Mr Tunstable had written, the was a lot of money that came with the property from rent for smaller houses on the estate for local families and the servants, as well as the leasing of land such as the small paddock on the edges of the property lines that housed the sheep for a local haberdasher.

He spent the whole of breakfast pondering what to do. Nobody joined him for the morning meal, so he had a lot of time to think.

Something about Miss Hartley had captured his mind, and he was tormented with conflicting emotions. Who did he side with? He had to keep Major Hartley friendly, but he knew he wouldn't be able to keep the secret from Miss Hartley. Perhaps if he could make peace with her, he could convince her to leave the Major alone and stop threatening his case.

By the time his plates had been cleared away, he had determined to talk to Miss Hartley. The way he saw it, if he listened to her theories and let her discover the right answer on her own, he wasn't really telling her anything, and he'd be doing as Major Hartley had ordered. Miss Hartley was a clever, headstrong woman. He was sure she was bound to figure it out. Right now, he just needed to find her.

He first went to the sitting room, hoping she might be there, but the room was empty. He checked the dining room and the parlour then surveyed the back garden from the upper floor before he was forced to ask the staff if they'd seen her.

"Where was she going?" Duncan asked impatiently.

"She . . ." The young boy paused and fiddled with the edge of his sleeves. "She doesn't want that information made known to you, sir."

Duncan sighed. He couldn't blame her, but now wasn't the time for her to be having a childish tantrum. He was going to do exactly what she'd asked.

"Did she go to town?" Duncan questioned.

Toby shook his head. "The Major has gone to town. Miss Beatrice wasn't with him."

"Well, do ye at least know when she'll be back?"

The young boy shook his head again.

"Ach. Well then, prepare ma horse," he instructed the boy. "If she is determined nae tae tell me where she is, I'll find her maself."

Toby didn't say anything, his expression looking torn. Eventually he nodded and left for the stables.

Meanwhile, Duncan changed into his riding clothes. When he got to the courtyard, his horse was ready and waiting. "Can ye at least give me a clue as tae where she's gone?"

The boy slowly raised his hand and pointed towards the right turn at the end of the drive.

Duncan thanked him and started along the path. He didn't gallop, but he didn't set a walking pace, either—he wanted to find her quickly, though he didn't want to ride straight past her.

After five minutes of riding, he saw a figure walking down the hill, a large bag hanging at her side. As he drew closer, he saw this was definitely Miss Hartley, so he called to her. He couldn't help but laugh as she turned, saw him and turned back, walking faster.

He quickly drew alongside her, but she kept walking.

"I told you not to talk to me," she stated, keeping her eyes fixed on the road ahead of her.

"Where are ye going, lass?" he called down.

"That's none of your concern," she snapped back.

"Why did ye nae take a horse?"

"I like walking." She paused. "And my mare has thrown a shoe."

"Easy tae remedy," Duncan pressed.

"The blacksmith is busy this week." She clearly didn't want to give him any information, but he persevered.

"What's in the bag?"

"Leave me alone."

Duncan pressed the horse forward and positioned himself across the road, blocking her path.

"Get out of my way." She stood strong, impatient and unyielding, refusing to look him in the eye.

"Yer obviously going somewhere with that bag. And there's nae a place in walking distance."

"Anywhere is within walking distance if you're not afraid of a long walk."

Duncan was tempted to jump down and simply lift her onto his horse. But if she didn't want him to talk to her, he was sure she wouldn't want him to touch her. "Aye," he replied cautiously. "But walking takes longer than riding."

Miss Hartley stopped. Duncan watched her think, and he knew the moment she'd decided he was right — her shoulders dropped in defeat, and she took a centring breath.

"Fine," she admitted. "But only because I care for my brother and his wife, not because I like you."

"Aye, fair enough." There was little more that Duncan could say, so he jumped down and helped Miss Hartley onto the horse. But she seemed rather shocked when he climbed on behind her.

"What are you doing?" she cried, twisting her neck to look at him.

Duncan chuckled. "I'm gonnae have tae come with ye. Bucephalus doesnae take kindly tae strangers riding him without me too. He'd buck ye off before ye could take hold of the reins."

"Bucephalus." Miss Hartley let out a dry laugh. "And I suppose you fancy yourself as Alexander the Great?"

"Naturally," Duncan replied, playing into the insult. In truth, the name had come from the horse's untameable nature. His uncle couldn't deny him learning to ride. Duncan's father had made provisions before he died, but Graeme made sure to make the experience as damned well difficult as he could. Duncan was given the most skittish and unsociable animal that terrorised the stables. The steed had been a bugger to work with. But with much time and effort, Duncan had finally come to form a partnership with him.

"So," Duncan asked cheerfully. "Where are we going?"

"Falton Bay," Miss Hartley offered begrudgingly.

"I'm going tae need a little more direction than that, lass."

The young woman stubbornly refused to say anything else but pointed down the path.

As they rode, Duncan could feel her tense. She was doing her level best not to touch him and not to relax around him. He knew she would get sore if she persisted in this manner, but he decided to leave her to it.

"So, yer visiting yer sister-in-law?" he asked conversationally, hoping to at least dampen the heavy silence.

"She's giving birth," Miss Hartley said plainly.

Duncan nodded his head and smiled. "I see. Is this her first bairn?" He happily noted Miss Hartley was starting to ease her position. He was sure her excitement would overtake her anger soon.

"Yes," she answered curtly. After a pause, she continued. "Annabelle is my younger brother's wife. They were married last year, and this is their first child."

"And is this younger brother as odd as the elder?" He was joking, but he'd misread her mood. Miss Hartley whipped her head around to glare at him. "Sorry," he said quickly.

Miss Hartley blew out a breath. "Jasper . . ." She stopped. Her head turned slightly, and Duncan knew she was gazing back at the castle. "He's a pain. He's very rude and arrogant. And he makes me so mad when he treats me like a child. But he's trying his best."

Duncan released the reins and gently squeezed Miss Hartley's hand.

Miss Hartley sighed and leant back slightly against him.

Nearly an hour passed before they arrived at Falton. After their little talk, they'd continued in relative silence, only broken when Miss Hartley would call out directions.

Eventually she pointed to a cottage close to the shoreline.

"There it is," she said in obvious relief.

As they came up the path, a young man emerged from the house. As soon as they'd dismounted, he enveloped Miss Hartley in a hug.

"I'm so glad you're here," the man exclaimed, taking her hand. "The doctor says I can't see her until the baby's born. But I think he might let you in."

Miss Hartley quickly rushed up the stairs, bag in hand. When she didn't descend moments later, Duncan assumed the doctor had allowed her to stay.

The young gentleman then turned to Duncan. "You'll have to excuse me," he apologised. "My excitement has taken up all the room in my mind, and I cannot recollect who you are."

Duncan held out a hand and the two men shook. "Dunnae worry, ye didnae know me before. I'm Duncan Mackenzie. I've been staying at Godshollow. While I was out riding this morning, I found Miss Hartley walking tae ye. As the Major had taken the carriage, leaving no indication of when he'd return, and as ma horse doesnae take well tae strangers riding him, I offered to accompany her. She told me yer her younger brother."

"I am. Charles Hartley, at your service. Thank you for bringing her. We've been expecting this day for weeks. Beatrice would have been devastated to miss the birth."

"Yer welcome."

"Can I get you a drink?" Mr Hartley asked politely. "I have some sherry, I think. I want to save the good wine until the baby comes."

"Aye, if ye dunnae mind, that would be good."

The two gentlemen made their way to the parlour and sat with their drinks, awaiting the new arrival.

Maybe ten minutes had passed when Miss Hartley joined them. She wore a beaming smile that lit up her face.

Mr Hartley jumped to his feet.

"How is Annabelle?" he asked frantically.

"She's doing well," she replied with a smile. "The doctor said she was fine, though it's far from being over yet. The baby is taking its time."

He was visibly relieved and set about putting his coat on. "Thank goodness. I need to go to the church briefly. I'll only be the other side of the garden. If anything happens whilst I'm gone, please come and get me."

"Of course." Miss Hartley kissed the top of her brother's head and he exited.

This left Duncan alone in the parlour with the young woman. A silence stretched out between them. To his surprise, Miss Hartley poured herself a large glass of sherry before sitting opposite Duncan.

For a moment, she sat in silence, just watching the amber liquid swirl as she moved the glass. He wondered briefly if she was expecting him to leave the room, which would be the proper thing to do, but she soon started talking. "Thank you for your assistance," she said at length.

Duncan smiled. "Yer welcome." He paused. "Does this mean I'm allowed tae talk tae ye now?"

She looked at him with a serious expression, her brows furrowed. "That depends on what you have to say."

He let another silence develop, waiting for her to speak first.

"I was right yesterday, wasn't I? When I said you were here to take Godshollow from Mr Daniels?" she eventually said.

"I cannae say."

"More secrecy?"

"It isnae in ma control, lass."

"I understand," she stated far too casually. "Only I had a very interesting discussion with Mrs Lutton this morning."

Duncan's heart missed a beat, though he tried his best to seem unaffected. "Oh, aye? This is Mrs Lutton of the ball?"

"Yes. She came to discuss just that, but our conversation was most illuminating. She told me that Mackenzie is the name of the family who built Godshollow. Isn't that a coincidence?"

"If ye say so."

Miss Hartley huffed. "Well, that set me thinking, you see. Adding that information to what you said last night, there weren't any other conclusions to draw except that you were here to claim the castle for your family. Am I right?"

Duncan didn't reply, though it was tough. As he'd hoped, she was right, but he couldn't confirm that in any meaningful way. He just had to focus on his papers, knowing his claim would be lost if he told her it even existed.

A silence grew again. For at least ten minutes, all that could be heard was Annabelle's shouts of effort as the labour progressed.

This was one of the oddest situations Duncan had ever found himself in. Under normal circumstances, the two of them alone together in a room would cause all sorts of scandal, but as it was, if any of the staff in Mr Hartley's house were inclined to gossip, there wasn't much they would be able to say. The two young people were at opposite ends of the room, their limited conversation being interrupted by painful screaming coming from above them.

This was not at all what he'd been expecting when he'd made his plans to come to Godshollow.

"You know, there's part of me that hopes you *are* here to take the castle." Miss Hartley commented, breaking another long silence. "Jasper will never say it, but he hates running an estate. He would have rather stayed in the army. When our father died, he was the one who had to take over."

"Could he nae have given it tae yer young brother?"

"Good heavens, no. Jasper will never actually admit something's too much for him. He's prideful and stubborn—he'd rather let the effort kill him than ask for help."

"Aye. Many men feel the same."

Miss Hartley shook her head. "Then they're all moronic," she lamented. "I love being at Godshollow, and I get on with the staff, which means I have a lot more information than Jasper does, but he never takes my advice. He wants to keep us all in our little boxes—him the provider, me the useless woman, and our brother the rector. I think that's why he liked the army so much. Everything had a strict hierarchy, and he wielded a lot of power."

Duncan took a mouthful of his drink to avoid answering. He had long experience of the ways power could corrupt a man and how it affected the people around him.

His silence was clearly too much for Miss Hartley to bear, as she tried to restart the conversation.

"So, what do you think of my theory, Mr Mackenzie?"

Duncan took another sip, then replied. "I think yer nae as angry as ye should be if ye really do think that's ma intention."

The corner of her mouth curled with a smile. "Don't worry. When I've had time to really think about it, I'm sure I'll be very cross."

She swallowed the remaining drops of her drink. She was certainly far from what Duncan had come to expect from an Englishwoman, and he couldn't say he was sorry about it.

"Does this mean you're not really in the circus?" she asked with a laugh.

"Aye, I'm afraid so."

"Mrs Lutton will be so disappointed."

Duncan laughed.

"I am too," she admitted candidly. "I've never met a circus performer before. I was hoping you might teach me a few tricks to give my rides a little more excitement."

Duncan's mind went blank. He couldn't formulate an appropriate response. There was something about her asking for excitement that overwhelmed his rational thinking. Watching her riding properly would be an exhilarating activity, he was sure—her hair wind-blown, her face flushed with exertion, her movements sharp and strong. His imaginings were interrupted when Mr Hartley returned from the church.

"Has anything happened?" He hurriedly peeled his gloves off.

"You haven't missed anything," Miss Hartley assured him.

"The only major change has been tae yer supply of sherry," Duncan commented jokingly.

"Ah," Mr Hartley replied with a smile. "So Jasper turned up then?"

"No," Miss Hartley replied. She let out a merry giggle. "Actually, I don't know where he is. No doubt he's with Mr Ocheridge, discussing how much of his debt will be paid off if he gives him my hand in marriage."

Such a bald-faced admission shocked Duncan. Marrying for money was a common enough situation, but he'd never heard such a trade talked about so plainly and openly, especially by the *intended bride* who was supposed to have very little to do with, never mind an understanding of, the situation. Hearing her speak on her worth as a bride really emphasised the personal cost of such arrangements. The idea that a man like Ocheridge would make a good husband for someone as strong and spirited as Miss Hartley was laughable really.

Who *would* be a good man for Miss Hartley? She'd need

someone who would help her grow rather than restrain her. Anyone who expected her to be a timid housewife was in for a shock. She would work well with a man who saw marriage as a partnership, one who would respect her and her opinions. She needed someone, essentially, who was the complete opposite of her brother and his lawyer friend.

She needed a man like Duncan.

That wasn't a *terrible* idea. He was certainly attracted to her, and he was sure she was attracted to him — especially if her reaction to him in his kilt was anything to go by. She was a passionate woman and fiercely independent, which Duncan preferred to the idea of a meek and subservient wife.

In addition, there was the added bonus that their marriage might well give him his future at Godshollow, should his claim be denied. If they were married, surely Major Hartley wouldn't leave his sister homeless, which was what Duncan would be if the claim fell through.

The beginnings of a plan were forming in his mind.

CHAPTER NINE

Beatrice woke in an unfamiliar room. Seconds passed before she began to remember the events of the night before and where she was. The day before had certainly been interesting.

She'd still been angry when she arose the previous morning, and her indignation only worsened when Mrs Lutton visited. Not because of her friend, of course, but rather the information she imparted. Mrs Lutton had come to deliver her husband's ideas about who Mr Mackenzie was.

General Lutton had recognised the name of Godshollow's guest immediately, explaining that Mackenzie was the name of the man who had built Godshollow in the 1600s. That had led Beatrice to the only possible conclusion she could draw — Duncan Mackenzie had come to Godshollow to claim the place for himself. In their part of the country, Scottish ancestry was very rare, and the area was by no means a tourist destination, so the fact that Mr Mackenzie shared a name with the builder of Godshollow was too big a coincidence to be ignored.

She had been furious, but everything had been pushed from her mind when Tobias came with the note from Falton saying that Anabelle was going into labour. The messenger had already gone to town to send word to Mr Daniels and Annabelle's parents by coach. When Beatrice saw Jasper had taken the carriage, she began to walk, and everything else passed from her mind.

Unfortunately, her peace hadn't lasted very long. When

Mackenzie had come across her, all of her frustration had been brought back. She found everything about him irritating, and having him there at Falton Bay was incredibly uncomfortable.

But this discomfort was pushed aside when the baby was finally born. She remembered vividly how the doctor had come down to announce the birth and then admitted Charles and Beatrice into the room to see Annabelle and meet the new baby.

Charles was ecstatic. He cuddled his son, regarding him as though he was as precious as the holy grail.

Beatrice watched the baby sleeping from over her brother's shoulder.

"He's beautiful, Annabelle," she congratulated her sister-in-law. Her nephew was so sweet and pure, Beatrice was overwhelmed with love for him.

Annabelle smiled weakly, tired out by her exertion. "Thank you," she replied, followed by a big yawn.

Beatrice kissed her sister-in-law on the forehead. "Well done, my darling." Then she turned to her brother. "I'll leave you three alone. When I get back to Godshollow, I'll make sure to send Jasper over as soon as I can."

Charles lifted his head and forced his gaze away from his son. "It's far too late for you to travel back now," he insisted. "You must stay here." Annabelle gently nodded her agreement. "Your room is always ready, and I'm sure I can find space for Mr Mackenzie. You can use our carriage to go home tomorrow. We're not going anywhere any time soon."

Beatrice eventually agreed. It was late, and she hadn't been looking forward to the journey in the dark. Charles's insistence that Mr Mackenzie stay as well was evidence of his giving, caring nature and proved why he was a good clergyman.

With the agreement that they would stay, Beatrice did as she promised and left the new family alone.

She went down to let Mr Mackenzie know about the plan for them to sleep there.

"I cannae intrude upon yer brother's hospitality that far," was his response. "I would need tae go separately in the morning tae take Bucephalus back anyway. I'll leave ye with yer family, ye dunnae need me here."

His words sounded harsh, but he had a point. In truth, it would have been considered outside of social guidelines for him to have stayed at all, but Charles had a generous soul.

And it seemed Mr Mackenzie had similar gentlemanly manners, which appealed to Beatrice. His reasons for being at Godshollow certainly were bad for her, but he was by no means a bad man. She wasn't sure if it was the euphoria of being an aunt or the sherry she'd drunk, but she felt her feelings towards Mr Mackenzie becoming warmer, more positive.

"Will you be able to get back in the dark?" she asked. "Can you remember the way we came?"

"Aye, lass," he replied. "The moon's bright and I'll stick tae the road. It's pretty much a straight line from here, and ye cannae miss Godshollow when yer driving up tae it."

Satisfied, Beatrice walked him to the stable to his horse.

"Thank you again for bringing me here," she expressed. She stepped out of the house and closed the door behind her to stop the cold air from going in.

"Yer welcome," he answered, with the same genuineness she'd heard the first time.

"Are you sure you'll be able to find the route?" she checked again.

Mr Mackenzie responded with a chuckle. "Aye. I'll be fine, dunnae ye worry. Now get back tae yer brother and the bairn." He took Beatrice's hand and pressed a kiss to it before he mounted his horse.

"Dunnae let the Major barter with yer future," he advised her seriously. "Yer worth a lot more than anything Mr Ocheridge could offer."

And with that he was gone.

She couldn't stop thinking about what Mackenzie had said.

She'd been thinking about it as she fell asleep and she was still thinking of it as she ate a quick breakfast with Charles.

She tried to put the words out of her head as she fussed over the new-born and checked on Annabelle's well-being, but what he'd said was a huge presence in her mind.

When she was finally alone in the carriage, being driven back to Godshollow, she could give his comment her full attention.

What had he meant by such a remark? Was he merely commenting that she was thinking too little of herself, or was he trying to imply that he thought of himself as being able to offer more? Mr Mackenzie was, without doubt, a handsome man—he looked particularly dashing in his kilt—and he wasn't the ill-tempered brute his arrival had made him appear to be. He seemed to like her and was very good at giving compliments, whether he meant them or not. Perhaps it wasn't an *awful* idea to view him as a potential suitor. He was certainly better than some of the men Jasper had suggested, and a definite improvement on Ocheridge.

There was also Godshollow to consider. Jasper had always wanted her to make a beneficial match, and what could be better than marrying the man who might end up in possession of their home? That would be a perfect way of ensuring that her family and Mr Daniels and Annabelle, who dearly loved the place, could still be able to visit the property even if they didn't own it anymore.

The more she thought about it, the more she thought it was a good idea. In the end, a marriage between herself and Mr Mackenzie would be what was best for everyone. The question was, should she talk to Jasper about her plan? Would he approve? Or would he tell her not to be so stupid and just do as she was told? How much money was riding on her marriage to Mr Ocheridge?

No. She couldn't tell him yet. Perhaps, if things moved

along as she hoped, she would explain it to him, but he didn't need to know about it now. Plus, if *he* was allowed to make plans about her future without consulting her, then she surely had the right to do the same with regard to him.

But she did need help. She had time constraints and she couldn't enact her plan alone. Her brother had sent the letter to Mr Daniels the day before, and even if he'd sent his fastest rider, it would still take at least two weeks for the letter to be delivered. Assuming that Mr Daniels left as soon as the note was received, altogether she had a month to secure a proposal from Mr Mackenzie.

And what better place to encourage romance than a ball?

When she arrived back at Godshollow, she quickly changed her dress and went down to the parlour. There she found her brother, but no Mr Mackenzie.

"Good morning, Jasper. I trust you were informed about the baby being born yesterday?"

"What are you talking about?"

"Charles and Annabelle's baby. He was born yesterday. Didn't you wonder where we'd gone?"

Jasper looked almost nervous for a moment, which captured her attention, but it was quickly replaced with suspicion. "We?"

"Mr Mackenzie offered his horse to help me get there." She tried to say this as nonchalantly as possible, but still Jasper wasn't impressed.

"That's odd. Because I distinctly remember a conversation wherein I told you to leave Mr Mackenzie alone. And he didn't mention it this morning at breakfast."

At least she now knew Mr Mackenzie had made it to Godshollow safely.

"It wasn't planned," Beatrice explained. "I received the message from Charles and started to walk there because you had taken the carriage. Mr Mackenzie must have been out for a ride on his horse when he spotted me. He offered to give me a ride."

"You could have refused."

Beatrice sighed. "It was just a trip to Falton. You're focussing on the wrong things here. You have a nephew, you should be excited."

"And I will be sending my congratulations," he replied. "But that doesn't mean you needed to get Mr Mackenzie involved."

Beatrice sighed and buttered some toast in order to focus her energy. "You know," she remarked casually. "You haven't *actually* given me a good reason not to speak to Mr Mackenzie."

Jasper arched an eyebrow at her and laid his paper down. He was gearing up for some long speech, she knew it.

"Beatrice," he began, his tone sharp and short. "I must say your recent behaviour has been very disappointing. I never remember you being this contrary with father."

That stung like a sharp jab in her chest. A lump formed in her throat, but she tried not to let it colour her reply. "I'm not being contrary," she said defensively. "I just want to know what's going on. I live here too, you know. Whatever happens affects me, which is something our father knew but you don't, apparently. Father used to talk to me. He treated me like a member of the family, not as part of the staff."

As though a river had burst its bank, she couldn't stop. They hadn't really spoken about their father since his funeral.

"I'm a member of this family, a person, not a commodity to be bargained with. You've been trying so hard to get me engaged because that's all you think I'm good for. Father wanted a good match for me as well, but he also prepared me for life after a wedding. He made sure that I became proficient in running a household.

"Whilst you were away in the army, I did a lot to help him

run the house. I'm much more useful than just my marriage potential. Did you know that it was *me* who organised the repair for the leak in the parlour? Did you even know there was one?"

"Of course, I—"

"I wasn't finished. I've done so much more than the pittance *you* think I'm able to do because *you* want to be completely in control of running the estate. Which is ridiculous, by the way, because we both know you'd rather be back in the army, even though you haven't been a major for over a year and a half. You'd think you'd let someone help who actually *wanted* to rather than being selfish with the responsibilities because you won't accept that someone is better than you at something. That's why I *behaved better* for our father, because he trusted me. He knew I was a capable, intelligent woman, and he *never* made me feel as though I was being excluded from this family."

Her heart was racing. She felt as though she'd run the entirety of the Godshollow grounds twice over. Her chest was heaving, and she knew her face was probably flushed with anger.

Jasper just sat with a dumb expression on his face, not a word passing his lips.

"Nothing?" Beatrice cried in exasperation. She felt humiliated. She'd just bared herself to him emotionally, and Jasper didn't seem to care. He couldn't even muster up enough respect for her to even try and deny what she'd said.

She stormed out of the room, knowing she'd been mere seconds away from giving him a well-deserved slap. But she didn't want him to be able to explain away her behaviour as hysteria. There was a fine line between being angry and being hysterical, and a slap would have tipped her over that line.

She marched from the breakfast room straight to the stables, overwhelmed and in need of advice.

She thought about talking to Charles and Annabelle, but they would be busy with the new baby and she didn't want to bother them. That, and she needed motherly care. Charles and Annabelle were wonderful when she went to them with problems, but right now she needed someone older and more experienced. Someone who would be able to share her burden.

This set in her mind to visit Mrs Lutton.

She knew it was socially frowned upon to visit someone without prior notice, but she was desperate. She had planned to write to her friend and visit the next day, discussing her plans about Mr Mackenzie, but Jasper had pushed her over the edge.

The stable boy helped her get the carriage ready—Jasper wasn't going to monopolise its usage today—and as soon as the driver arrived, she was on her way.

The ride to Havenbrooke gave her time to let out her emotions and gently calm and come back to herself. Not that it did much good in the end. As soon as she saw Mrs Lutton, Beatrice broke down in tears.

Her wonderful friend put a comforting arm around her shoulders and led her into the house.

As a maid prepared tea, Beatrice poured her heart out to Mrs Lutton. She didn't realise how much she'd been bottling inside of herself. Not only did she explain the fight with Jasper, and Mr Mackenzie's intentions regarding Godshollow, she also cried about her father's death, how Annabelle's trauma had affected her, and her guilt at being affected by it. She bemoaned her spinsterhood and explained a general feeling of loss of control on a scale she'd never before encountered.

"I'm sorry," she said as she dabbed at her eyes with a handkerchief after the worst of the ranting was over. "I didn't mean for that to happen."

"But you certainly needed it," Mrs Lutton observed. "You're putting far too much pressure on yourself—anyone would crumble under the weight of your burdens. You're an amazing young woman to be sure, but nobody is expecting *that* much from you."

Beatrice worried the edges of the damp handkerchief between her fingers. "I just feel that no one else will worry about these things if I don't. Take Mr Mackenzie, for example. Jasper refuses to tell me what's going on, which would lead me to think Mr Mackenzie's business *is* a big issue, even if I didn't already know what it was. But when he's with Mr Mackenzie, it's as though there's nothing going on at all. Like he isn't thinking about the implications of Mr Mackenzie's claim and what would happen to us if he were to be successful."

She wasn't entirely sure that her explanation made any sense, but she *was* sure there was something off about Jasper's behaviour. That, or she was going crazy. Mrs Lutton's response would hopefully provide her an answer.

"It's all very odd, isn't it? It could be that your brother doesn't want you getting hurt. Or maybe he's so certain Mr Mackenzie won't succeed that he doesn't have to worry. But you're right, his behaviour *is* questionable."

"I admit that I'm not knowledgeable about property law, or whether Mr Mackenzie's claim has potential. But even if Jasper *was* certain the claim wouldn't result in anything, his behaviour is still extraordinary.

She paused for a moment, again pulling at her handkerchief. "For example, he was very defensive when I asked if he'd written to Mr Daniels about Mr Mackenzie coming to speak to him. I know my brother. The harder he tries to assert something, the more he's lying about it. Something's not right."

"I don't *want* to think badly of him," she felt compelled to add, even as she continued to worry at the delicate linen.

"I know, dear, I know," Mrs Lutton said soothingly. "Nevertheless, he shouldn't have treated you like that. Nobody would blame you if he wasn't your favourite person right now. People might expect Mackenzie to be at the bottom of your list of positive acquaintances. But from what you told me of last night, I suspect he might be considerably higher up. I tell you, I'm put in mind of *The Barest Heiress*."

Beatrice couldn't help but laugh. "I didn't know you read Fanny Sparrow," she remarked with surprise.

Mrs Lutton chuckled. "It's a recent development. Do you remember after Annabelle's ordeal she refused to read any of those books she loved so much?"

Beatrice did. Her heart had broken to watch Annabelle physically panic when she tried to read one of her beloved stories. She couldn't even cope if Charles read to her and she was safely tucked against his side. Charles had taken every single volume out of their home.

"Well, your lovely brother had a suspicion that dear Annabelle might recover and want the books back. So he asked me to take them into my care. He knew you also had copies, but he also understands the importance and emotion of a personal book collection.

"Anyway, while they've been under my protection, I decided to see what all the fuss was about."

"Did you enjoy them?"

"Far too much."

Laughter filled the room, but the humorous reprieve was brief.

Beatrice took a deep breath. "Jasper might not be thinking about our future at Godshollow, but I am. I think I've come up with a plan."

Of course, Mrs Lutton had some trepidations about the plan, but none of her doubts questioned Beatrice's intelligence.

"It's admirable you would even consider something like this for the sake of your family, but I'm sure it won't come to that."

"It's best to plant the seeds now. Who knows? I may grow to love him."

"And if you don't? Will you be able to sacrifice your happiness to commit to a man you don't know? He may have many flaws that will only come to light once it is too late."

"Yes."

Mrs Lutton nodded her head resolutely. "Indeed. Well, if there's anything I can do to help, let me know."

Beatrice thought for a moment. "Now that you mention it, I do have a few ideas. You mentioned adding some Scottish flare to the decorations for your ball?"

Chapter Ten

The day after the bairn's birth, Duncan awoke far from rested. Sleep had not been forthcoming, and any repose he'd managed to have was disturbed and confused.

None of this was what he'd pictured when he'd left Scotland.

He'd never imagined encountering anyone like Miss Hartley. Besides his nanna, he'd never known anyone so inherently good.

At the birth, he'd seen her true nature — the caring, kind, devoted sister, with a wonderful sense of humour and sparkling wit and intelligence. Now that he'd had a chance to talk to her, he knew the anger and bitterness she'd exhibited thus far were not her ordinary way, not who she wanted to be. He could hardly blame her for acting in such a manner.

This was what kept him awake. He was genuinely attracted to her and couldn't stop thinking about her. His plan of suggesting himself as a suitor for Miss Hartley wouldn't be difficult in that respect. In fact, he would probably pursue Miss Hartley even if she couldn't ensure he would be able to stay at Godshollow.

However, he was irritatingly conflicted about the whole idea. Wrestling with his morals also helped to chase sleep from him. He knew he'd be considered caddish if he manoeuvred a woman into a marriage against her express wishes, so he wanted to know if that was actually a worthwhile thing to do.

When a clock in the hallway struck four o'clock, he knew

he was never going to get any sleep, and he resolved to visit his lawyer in town. He dressed quickly and went outside, hoping that fresh air might help him wake.

Not until he was on the road did he realise he didn't know exactly where he was going. He knew vaguely what direction the town was in, as he'd passed it on his way to Godshollow, but he'd been cold and wet and tired, and his memory was far from crystal clear. Luckily, the number of roads available was limited, and where he had to choose between paths, he found roadside markers to help.

When he got into the town, he was again lost, as he didn't know where the lawyer's office was. He'd written the address numerous times, he could recite it from memory, but that wouldn't help him find the street he was looking for.

He dismounted his horse and tied him up in a communal stable on the edge of the town, then set off walking down the streets, hoping the office wouldn't be too far.

As it was, the town was very ramshackle. No two buildings were the same — the current fashion for uniformity and cohesion in town planning clearly hadn't reached this part of the country yet. This was clearly a town that had built up gradually over the years, one street being built maybe even a century after the one adjacent to it. And it had a patchwork of buildings all made from whatever was the *fashionable* brick at the time.

He finally arrived at Widdersham & Ocheridge a little after half past six, having spent half of an hour wandering a maze of streets and alleyways, feeling as though he'd covered just as much ground on foot as his hour's ride to the town.

Once he saw the building, he knew he'd arrived at the right place. Tall and imposing, the brick had been painted a dull grey and had been built at the end of an older row. The building was ugly, and certainly didn't help to minimise the convention that lawyers were dark, soulless people.

He knocked on the door. Swinging it open was an unhappy looking older woman, no doubt hired specifically for answering the door and greeting customers.

"Are you Mr Williams?" she asked curtly.

"Nae, ma'am."

"Then Mr Widdersham and Mr Ocheridge are not available until eight o'clock today," she reported in a flat, monotone, a drone. Her message given, she tried to shut the door, but Duncan put his hand in the way.

"And Tunstable?"

The woman shook her head. "Ain't nobody here with that name. It's too early for running the rig, now go away."

This time she successfully slammed the door in his face.

Duncan stood on the top step a moment. His tired mind hadn't completely realised what had just happened. When his stomach growled loudly, he decided perhaps he'd be better off trying again at a later hour. Whilst he waited, he might as well get some breakfast.

Luckily, his nose led him to a pub around the corner at the other end of the street that was clearly serving early clientele. A plume of grey smoke rose from the chimney. Busy servants bustled through the doors, opening windows, and doing their general daily tasks.

The pub was surprisingly light. Most establishments like this that Duncan had visited were dark and dingy, but this was bright and clean, its open, pleasant atmosphere clearly popular, as there was a reasonable patronage already there.

After Duncan made his way to the bar, the barman took his order for breakfast and coffee and then took payment.

As he found a table, he could hear wisps of people's conversations. One group in particular caught his interest. At the table next to him sat a portly man with an outrageous moustache, and a balding, red-cheeked fellow. They were having a loud conversation, even though they sat right next to each other.

"I don't know why, but it's all women are talking about these days," remarked one to the other.

"You don't have to tell me," replied the second man. "It's all Harriet will discuss. Every dinner time she tells me all of the exploits of an Arthur Avonlea fellow or whatever his name is. I tell you, if I ever meet this Fanny Sparrow, I have a few choice words for her."

"As have I. Margaret has been particularly taken by this *Humble Highlander* series. It's all a load of drivel, but she's determined she will marry a Scotsman."

Duncan was curious enough to want to ask the men what they were talking about, but after the first man's indignation about his — daughter? Ward? Sister? — wanting to marry a Scot, he decided against it.

Eventually, from what else he overheard whilst he was eating, he figured they were talking about some author. But why were they so annoyed by her? That was a question which would have to be answered later, because the clock in the inn showed eight o'clock.

Duncan made his way back to the law office, hoping the woman was right about the working hours.

At a quarter past eight, Duncan knocked once again on the dark door of the bleak house, which was opened by the same woman. Clearly, she remembered him.

"Back again? I told you there's no Tunstable here."

Duncan pushed forwards, giving the woman no choice but to let him in. "I know. I want tae speak with Ocheridge," he stated.

The woman sighed defeatedly and called after him as she shut the door. "Upstairs, first room on the right." As he left her behind, Duncan was sure he heard her mumble something about not being paid enough.

Duncan followed the directions and found his way to

Ocheridge's office. Just as he was about to let himself be known with a knock, Mr Ocheridge came barrelling out of the room, shouting to the maid.

"Who was at the door, Miriam? Oh! Mr Mackenzie." The last part had been practically shrieked as Duncan's presence took the lawyer by surprise.

"Good morning, Mr Ocheridge. Pleasure tae see ye again." As Duncan looked down on the man, he felt confident *he* was a better choice for Miss Hartley. Ocheridge was a toad-like man with pale, clammy skin and slightly bulging eyes. He looked slimy to the degree that Duncan wanted to wash just for having looked at him. He was not the good-looking man a woman deserved to have on her arm.

"Yes, yes," Ocheridge answered awkwardly – apparently, socialising really wasn't his forte.

"I've come tae speak tae Tunstable," Duncan began. "But yer … Miriam seems tae think he isnae here."

Ocheridge laughed. "Of course he is," he said quickly. "Poor Miriam gets confused sometimes. Her mind's not what it used to be. I should really look for a replacement."

"I dunnae think –"

"I say, hang on a moment. How silly of me. I'm coming to Godshollow this evening. You needn't have come all this way. We can talk tonight."

Duncan shook his head. "I'd rather speak with Tunstable, if it's all the same tae ye. He's the one who's been handling ma case."

"Of course, of course," Ocheridge pacified. "But you see, ah, Mr Tunstable is rather busy at the moment and I doubt he will be able to see you today. Are you sure I can't help with that question?"

That was something Duncan wanted to avoid. There would be no good asking about matrimonial law with a man he suspected was his rival for the lady in question. Ocheridge wouldn't take long to figure out who he was talking about, and Duncan didn't put it past him to lie in order to deter him from seeking Miss Hartley.

"I'm afraid it needs tae be Tunstable. I'm sure yer a very capable lawyer, but ye dunnae know ma case."

Mr Ocheridge's expression let Duncan know he'd succeeded in convincing him he wouldn't leave until he'd spoken to Tunstable. The lawyer rubbed the back of his neck and clicked his tongue.

"Wait here," he commanded. "I'll see if Tunstable has a spare minute for you." Then he disappeared upstairs. When he reappeared several moments later, he seemed calmer.

"George can see you now," he informed Duncan. He turned on his heel and led Duncan to the office, making Duncan wonder what all the fuss had been about in the first place.

Ocheridge knocked on the door and pushed it open. "You'll have to be brief. He's got a *lot* of work to be doing." Then he left them alone.

As it was, Tunstable didn't look all that busy. He was staring out a window, perhaps taking in the view.

Duncan took a minute to regard him.

Tunstable was more youthful than he expected. Duncan had expected a grey-haired man with a wrinkled brow and aged skin, but this man had an uninterrupted mass of dark blond hair and carried very few wrinkles. Perhaps the years had been much kinder to Mr Tunstable than they had been to anyone else. Maybe this was the son of the original Mr Tunstable. Or, and most likely, Duncan had completely misjudged the man's age from his writing—Mr Tunstable had every right to be a younger man.

However, the most striking thing about him could only be described with the word untidy. Nothing about him seemed neat or orderly, ink stains on his fingers, to the ruffled hair that was in dire need of a comb.

"Ah, Mr Mackenzie. Wonderful to meet you in person." He gripped Duncan's hand far too tightly and shook it with a vigour that Duncan hadn't expected. "Do have a seat."

Duncan looked about the room. It was just as disorganised as its owner. Assorted papers littered every available surface, covered in ink blotches and splashes of tea and biscuit crumbs. The books on the shelves were shoved in wherever there was space. A pile was stacked precariously in a corner, and what appeared to be an almanac propped up one leg of the desk.

Deciding it would be too much effort to tidy up the mess piled on the chair Tunstable had pointed to, he stood awkwardly next to a bookcase. He feared leaning on it too forcefully, as it appeared precariously balanced and he didn't want to topple it.

Tunstable looked about him, searching but finding nothing.

"Aha!" he exclaimed at length, pulling some papers from under a large pile and sending documents flying in every direction. He shook the page and flattened it out on the desk. "Here we are, yes?" He handed Duncan the paper.

"The papers dunnae matter so much right now. I just have a query," Duncan cut in impatiently, growing tired of the man's bumbling.

Tunstable relaxed and ceased the further muddling of his documents.

"Yes, of course. How can I help you?"

"Well, I'm here because I want tae know ma rights if I amnae given Godshollow."

"Oh!" the man exclaimed. "That's easy. If you are not granted the ownership of Godshollow, then you cannot have it."

"Aye," Duncan said slowly, trying not to get angry. "I'd figured that part. But what if I was married tae a member of the household? Would I be able tae stay?"

Tunstable's eyes widened in confusion. "I don't under-stand what you mean?" he said gingerly.

"It isnae a difficult question," Duncan responded, his tol-erance getting weaker by the second. "If I were tae marry, say, the lady of the house, would I be able tae live there even if I didnae get the property?"

Tunstable hemmed and hawed.

Duncan was beginning to wonder if it would be easier just to find a new lawyer.

"If ye dunnae know the answer, I can—"

"No, no," Tunstable assured him. "I'm just assessing your query, it's a very complicated issue." His response was an ob-vious placation, but Duncan was curious to see what would happen next. "I mean, don't you have a house of your own to live with your wife?"

"Oh aye. That's why I'm trying tae prove legal ownership of another's house," he replied sarcastically. "It's a simple aye or nae, lad. Do I have a better chance of being able tae stay at Godshollow if I had a legal relationship with one of the ten-ants?"

"Aye," Tunstable answered with a nod. "I mean yes. I think that it will ultimately be up to the owner, though a marriage would give you more leverage, I suppose."

That was uncertain, but it was more than Duncan had at four o'clock that morning.

"Thank ye," Duncan said. "Good day, Mr Tunstable."

The young man stood to shake his hand and sent another pile of papers tumbling to the floor. He looked sheepishly at Duncan.

"Goodbye Mr Mackenzie. Again, a pleasure to meet you, at long last."

Duncan nodded. He just wanted out of that office. He felt as though the untidiness had made *him* dirty just by standing in it.

As he left the office, something wasn't sitting in Duncan's stomach quite right.

He'd expected more from the man he'd been corresponding with for so long. There was certainly a discrepancy between the Tunstable of the letters and the Tunstable he'd met. Then again, it was easy to seem different in a letter when one had time to compose what was to be said and other people could read it over. Duncan had somewhat surprised the man with the visit — even though he had suggested to Ocheridge that one was coming — perhaps he was being too hard on the man.

He would be interested to find out that night how much Ocheridge had been told of Duncan's questions, if he was involved with the case — his proximity to the Hartleys and to Godshollow gave him a vested interest in Duncan's activities. He wanted to know what was going on in that office. If Ocheridge was being told everything by Tunstable, Duncan needed to be careful about the information he made available to others. He did not want Ocheridge more involved with this case than he already was.

This added even more pressure to his decision to make an offer to Miss Hartley. If Ocheridge was aware of his plans, he'd no doubt do anything he could to disrupt them. With that in mind, Duncan had to get back to Godshollow and begin his wooing. He had to win Miss Hartley before she resigned herself to Ocheridge, plus uncover what was making him so uneasy about his business with the law firm before he ran out of time.

When he returned to the castle, Duncan was informed Miss Hartley had gone for a walk. Winning her over would be very hard if she was always out.

He thought for a moment about going out to find her but

decided to do some investigating. Anything he could find to help him understand Miss Hartley would be invaluable, especially as the Major seemed determined to keep her from talking to him and giving him the information herself.

Asking anyone in the house about her would be useless. Major Hartley would find such inquiries all too suspicious and untoward, which could jeopardise his chances of spending more time with Miss Hartley should he have to relocate to a hotel.

He would have to see which of her possessions he could find about the house and hope they would give him some insight. He just needed to figure out where to start.

Perhaps this was an opportunity to explore Godshollow, to take a tour and find out what he could about Miss Hartley along the way. The Major seemed determined that Miss Hartley wasn't to talk to Duncan, so he'd have to explore different ways of getting to know her.

He felt guilty at first, always turning the servants away if they found him wandering the halls, but in the end, he justified it to himself that it was in her best interest as well. Surely a potential partner who knew and understood her personality was preferable to one who cared nothing about her interests.

After about half an hour of wandering, he found himself outside of yet another bedroom. So far, he'd encountered many rooms that as appeared to be bedchambers, but they'd all been disappointing. Some of them were locked so could offer Duncan nothing. Some had been used — most likely used for guests after a ball or party — but showed no signs of a personal touch. In the year that Mr Daniels had owned the property, it would be impossible for his tenants not to have left some signs of their unique style in the rooms they used most. Like most of the other bedrooms, the door to this one was already open, so Duncan once again went inside, though his hope of finding anything useful had been dwindling with each failure.

However, this choice proved more fruitful.

This room was inhabited. It was lived in. There was no fire burning at that time, but the fireplace had clearly been recently used. The ash and coal hadn't been swept, suggesting that the fire had been lit to keep the occupant warm while they dressed, and the servants hadn't been in yet to lay the fire for the evening. The window shutters were wide open — in the unused rooms these had been closed. A shelf and a dresser held books and sewing items, along with small trinkets that were not simply put there for decoration but were used by their owner — no dust had collected on the shelf where they sat, and they were positioned slightly crooked, as if they'd been picked up and put back down rather than placed specifically and carefully for display. This room had to be Miss Hartley's. No servant would have such a grand room — he hadn't yet found the servants' quarters — and the necklaces, hair ribbons and perfume bottle on the dressing table suggested a woman, so it was not Major Hartley's room.

A book lay atop the neatly arranged bed covers, a battered bookmark peeking out. Duncan picked up the book, fingering the red ribbon of the bookmark. He wondered how many other books the worn material had been used for.

Opening the book, Duncan found the name of the author, Fanny Sparrow, followed by the title, *Her Own Soldier*.

The name brought a memory to the front of Duncan's mind. This was what the men had been talking about in the pub that morning. The books women were obsessed with at the moment. Perhaps he would see what was of such great interest.

He turned the pages to the section held by the bookmark and began to read.

"We will surely be caught," she whispered frantically as Sebastian pulled her into the alcove behind the tapestry of Salome and

John the Baptist.

"Let them find us. I could not bear another second without you."
The guardsman had his hands on her, holding her, grasping her like
a dice-man grasps his last hope.

"But the prince will have your head if he hears of this."

"You are worth the risk, my lady. When I saw you enter, I could
not contain my passions. You are divine. Your beauty is such that
it would make Cleopatra cry, and make Paris's Helen a mere bar-
wench by comparison."

He pressed her against the wall, his lips hungrily moving over
her skin. She longed to cry out, as the pleasure she felt was immeas-
urable.

He shut the book quickly. No wonder these tales were causing complaints. He'd expected some sort of romance, judging by the men's comments at the inn, but this was much more unequivocal than he was prepared for, giving rise to *feelings* he wasn't prepared for.

He became excited to think that she read this sort of literature. How would she look as she let the story entrance her? Would she recline, relaxed, as she let it wash over her? Or would she lean forward, her nose nearly touching the page, as she tried to get as close to the story as possible?

This train of thought alerted him to the invasion of privacy he was committing. He dropped the book as if it were a burning coal.

But shame didn't snuff out that spark of thrill that had been lit. He wondered if there were any more of these books around the house, something that Miss Hartley wasn't reading that he wouldn't find so intimately connected to her.

That had been his plan, at least, but when the clock struck twelve o'clock, Duncan realised he was hungry. He abandoned his search for more books and made his way to the kitchen—he was uncertain he would last until two o'clock, when lunch was served. On his way, he came across Miss

Hartley, who had apparently returned from her walk.

His breath caught in his throat when he saw her. She was windswept and red-cheeked, just as he'd imagined. She looked wonderful.

Yes, he wouldn't regret pursuing this beautiful woman. He was almost knocked off of his feet when she looked up at him and gave him a dazzling smile.

"Mr Mackenzie, I hope you're well today." Taking off her gloves, she held a hand out to him.

He took it without thinking and kissed it.

They stood for a moment in silence, as Miss Hartley took on a more embarrassed demeanour.

"I must thank you so much for your help yesterday," she told him. She was watching him carefully, and Duncan remembered the last thing he'd said to her.

Yer worth a lot more than anything Mr Ocheridge could offer.

"It wasnae any trouble," he replied. He tried to reduce the tension between them with a reassuring smile. He'd often been told he had a strong smile, a heart-melting smile, and he hoped she would think that was true.

"Well," she responded after a moment. "I am nonetheless in your debt and eternally grateful."

Duncan bowed his head modestly to her in thanks. "Is that where ye've been? Seeing the bairn?"

Something flashed in Miss Hartley's eyes that Duncan couldn't quite figure out.

"Not exactly. I noticed you were out this morning," she commented. "Did you have fun?"

"Nae exactly," Duncan replied, parroting her answer back to her with a small wink.

A subtle blush tinted her cheeks.

"Would ye join me fer a cup of tea?" he asked hopefully.

Her face lit up,, but quickly turned downcast. "That's a lovely idea, though I'm afraid I have things to do. Mr Peters has just informed me Mr Ocheridge is dining with us *again* this evening, so I had best spend my time making myself *presentable,* as Jasper calls it." She tipped her head to one side thoughtfully and pushed out an exhale of breath. She leant towards him conspiratorially.

"To be honest," she said in a low voice. "I'd much rather let them eat by themselves."

"I dunnae blame ye."

She gifted him a small curtsey and began to walk away.

On instinct, he called after her. "Ye *can* do better than him, ye know." That was bold. He was risking a lot, but he couldn't help himself.

Miss Hartley turned to him, the corner of her mouth quirking into a secretive smile. "We'll see."

CHAPTER ELEVEN

Beatrice felt empowered. She had never so openly flirted with a man in her life, and that gave her a great rush of excitement. Or perhaps that was just Mr Mackenzie? The look on his face when he'd greeted her had been so uplifting.

She hadn't lied. She would much rather have tea with him than dine with her brother and Mr Ocheridge. Her stomach fluttered to think of his reply.

Ye can do better than him, he'd told her. And how his eyes had burned with intrigue and eagerness when she had as good as told him she wanted him to prove it.

As she brushed her hair out and curled it into a more formal evening style, hands trembling with excitement, she realised this was definitely about more than just remaining at Godshollow. Mrs Lutton had asked her if she could still go through with a marriage if she found him intolerable, but she had the strong suspicion that wouldn't be a problem.

Having known him for only four days, she was certain he was *at least* more companionable than Mr Ocheridge — funny, witty, and able to hold a conversation that wasn't about himself. And to top it off, he was a fair amount better looking than his opponent.

Perhaps it was as Mrs Lutton suggested, and Beatrice was willing things to be comparable to a romance novel. But even if she was, wasn't she allowed a little fantasy? Why should she give up the hope of a love match just because she was a little older?

She appreciated Mrs Lutton's support. Her friend had

promised to make the ball a romance-inspiring event. This could really be the chance Beatrice had never dared wish for.

She was determined to get to know Mr Mackenzie better, Jasper be damned. She'd find any excuse to talk to him and, preferably, be alone with him.

That was going to be tricky. Jasper really hadn't been happy about their ride to Falton, though perhaps her outburst had made him rethink things. Expecting Jasper to see things from her perspective was a long shot, but stranger things had happened.

She hadn't seen her brother since she'd returned home. Perhaps she should be the one to offer the olive branch, but it seemed as though she always was doing that. It was his turn now. Her decision to pursue Mr Mackenzie had unearthed a self-confidence in her she'd forgotten she had. She'd always been headstrong and outspoken, but she really felt as though she was taking charge of her life for once. The power was intoxicating.

As usual, at six o'clock she made her way to the dining room for dinner. Jasper and Mr Ocheridge were already there, brandy in hand, engaged in a conversation

"That's what he said," Mr Ocheridge was saying animatedly.

"Can that be allowed?" Jasper responded incredulously. "If I don't consent? I'm her guardian. Perhaps we should bring the plan forwards . . ."

That was when Ocheridge noticed Beatrice had joined them and he stopped the conversation. He came across the dining room, hand outheld to take hers.

"Miss Hartley," he addressed her loudly, followed by a grandiose bow. "You look" — he paused, no doubt searching his tiny mind for an interesting adjective — "pulchrous."

That was certainly an interesting word. Beatrice had never

heard it before and had no idea what it meant—she'd be surprised if Ocheridge did either. He certainly seemed the type of man to use obscure words in order to make himself sound intelligent without fully understanding what they meant. His efforts of appearing worldly and cultured were undermined by Mr Mackenzie's entrance.

"I'm sure I heard a farmer use that word tae describe a ewe once."

Beatrice desperately tried not to laugh, but a short, high giggle burst through the gaps in the fingers that covered her mouth. She couldn't tell if Mr Mackenzie was just being facetious, or whether he was actually being honest, but the effect on Ocheridge was impressive.

Mr Ocheridge went red in the face and started to become flustered. He began spluttering and tripping over his own tongue as he tried to explain he'd never heard it used in that context. His response told Beatrice that Ocheridge really didn't know exactly what the word meant in the first place, and his reaction just made her laugh harder. Jasper gave Beatrice a look which clearly meant he expected her to say something, but nothing came to mind.

She laid a consoling hand on Mr Ocheridge's arm, pushing down her revulsion of him.

"Thank you, Mr Ocheridge," she said awkwardly. "I appreciate the thought."

She could think of nothing else to say, and she could tell Jasper wasn't impressed by her feeble attempt to avoid showing preference for Mr Mackenzie.

Mr Mackenzie, on the other hand, gave her a cheeky smile.

Fortunately, they were interrupted by the arrival of dishes. The conversation lulled as they took their seats and began to eat. But inevitably the talking began again, with Mr Ocheridge trying to outshine Mr Mackenzie's natural charm with a dazzling display of belittling pompousness.

"I'm glad Mr Tunstable was able to help you today. Though he was surprised at having to answer *such* a simple question."

"Oh, aye?" Mr Mackenzie replied with easy coolness. "Are ye sure it was me he was talking about? He had a bit of trouble remembering ma name."

Another point to Mr Mackenzie. Beatrice considered keeping score on paper, though she suspected the amusement would quickly turn to second-hand embarrassment when it was clear the game was very one-sided. Also, she couldn't help but throw her support behind her favourite.

"Mr Mackenzie?" she asked sweetly, ignoring Jasper's glares for speaking to one whom she was forbidden to address. "If I might be so bold, might I enquire as to your Christian name? Charles and Annabelle are looking for a name for their little boy, and I've heard Scottish names are beautiful."

Jasper nearly choked on his soup spoon as he inhaled with shock. "Beatrice," he barked madly. "That is *not* an acceptable question."

"I dunnae mind," Mr Mackenzie cut in. "Ma name's Duncan. Though I dunnae know how *beautiful* it is."

A lovely name that suited him. A strong name, bulky and powerful, like him—she wouldn't have said that in front of her brother, though.

Mr Ocheridge tried to butt his way in again. "Would you like *my* Christian name, Miss Hartley? It may not be Scottish, but my family has only the best names, everyone says so."

"That's very kind of you," Beatrice lied. "But I think they're looking for Scottish names, really."

"Don't be ridiculous," Jasper imposed. "I'm sure they want a good *English* name, like the rest of us. I have no doubt they would be overjoyed to have a name from such a prestigious family as Mr Ocheridge's. Pray tell what is it?"

Ocheridge smiled haughtily. "Archibillious."

The room went silent. Beatrice had to muster all her strength not to burst into loud, raucous laughter. Instead she asked, "What a . . . *unique* name. Where does it come from?" As much as she had no desire to delve into Mr Ocheridge's life, she *had* to know where such a ridiculous name came from.

"It's a family name," he answered with pride. "It was my father's name, and his father before him, and his father before him. If I ever have children, all my male progeny will bear the name—excuse me, is there something wrong, Mr Mackenzie?"

Beatrice looked to the Scotsman, who seemed to be racked with a coughing fit, though not a very convincing one.

"Nae. Thank ye," he said once he'd acted the charade long enough. He took a deep breath and then excluded himself from the conversation by taking a drink from his cup.

The rest of the meal was rather much of a muchness. Mr Ocheridge would make an ignorant comment and the other diners tried not to laugh at him. There were moments when even Jasper must have realised his friend was making a fool of himself.

Unlike the occasion of their last meal together, Jasper and Mr Ocheridge stayed with Beatrice and Mr Mackenzie when the dining was over. But before they could all enter the parlour room, Jasper took Beatrice aside.

"I've been thinking," he said as he stopped her from entering the parlour. "I think that perhaps I was hasty in telling you not to talk to Mackenzie. You may, naturally, be as civil as society requires, but I don't want you being overly friendly. There, I have shown myself the bigger man and allowed a compromise. Now you have to start being willing to do the same. I can't have you disobeying me all the time. You have *got* to start being submissive to others. You'll make a poor wife otherwise."

"Unbelievable," Beatrice uttered in shock. "You really think it was your best plan to tell me that? Did you listen to nothing I said this morning?"

"Of course I did. You said father used to teach you how to be a wife, not just a bride, and this is me doing the same." His tone implied he couldn't believe she hadn't accepted his comments.

"You're incredible," she seethed. "I'm going for a walk in the garden." She prodded an angry finger into his chest and lowered her voice to an angry whisper. "And don't you *dare* send *Ocheridge the Odious* to follow me. I am *not* in the mood."

"You'd be lucky to have a man like Mr Ocheridge, you ungrateful brat," Jasper replied in similarly hushed tones.

"I'd rather marry a baboon." She said that slightly louder, then marched away, slamming the garden door as hard as she could.

Fresh air helped to calm her. As it filled her lungs, it pushed out all the bile clogging her chest. Jasper was unbelievable. No. Sadly, he was being altogether *too* believable. She only had herself to blame for expecting him to be reasonable regarding her little outburst.

She took a seat on the little wooden bench beside the fruit-tree-filled Orangery.

Tilting her head back, she watched the stars and tried to see things from Jasper's point of view. This was a mental exercise she found herself doing quite often. And now she had to do it again. She needed to calm down and at least *try* to understand Jasper before she could go back inside and pretend to be contrite and humble.

Her exercise in compassion took a little longer than usual. The problem wasn't that she couldn't understand his thinking, but that accepting those reasons was taking extra time.

When she finally returned inside, she found everyone had gone to bed. She tried not to feel upset that Jasper hadn't sought her out to say goodnight after their argument, but at least she had a little more time to prepare her fake apology.

She went to the servants' quarters and asked for hot water to be sent up for a bath. She found pouring a bath very soothing and asked that the servants bring the water and leave it outside of her room. The idea had been met with resistance at first, but eventually her maid was happy to let Beatrice do it herself.

She climbed the stairs to her room, trying to imagine Jasper's bumbling excuses to his bumbling friend about her hasty exit. No doubt there was some ridiculous adage about the inadequacy of the female mind and a woman's changeable temperament.

When she opened the door, she stepped on a little slip of paper that had been pushed through. She picked it up and unfolded it, revealing a quick sketch of a monkey in a top hat and cravat. Underneath was a little scribbled note. She could almost hear his Scottish accent as she read it.

It isnae a baboon, but still better looking than Ocheridge.

CHAPTER TWELVE

The next week did not go well. Tensions were high and the atmosphere was brittle, threatening to snap at any moment, like a bow string pulled taut by a man who couldn't hold it much longer.

Jasper's attitude towards Mr Mackenzie had completely reversed. Where he had seemed almost happy to have the stranger with them before, now he was hospitable only to the barest minimum. Beatrice couldn't understand Jasper's motives in all of this. As cold as he was to their guest, Jasper seemed desperate to keep Mr Mackenzie at Godshollow. Under the circumstances, anyone would have expected him to keep the man as far away as possible.

He also insisted on being present whenever Beatrice and Mr Mackenzie might have an opportunity to talk to each other. As if that wasn't bad enough, Mr Ocheridge was dining with them nearly every night. Their shared mealtimes became farcical, dominated as they were by Jasper and Ocheridge, who even forwent *eating* to make sure Beatrice and Mr Mackenzie had no opportunity to get a word in.

Beatrice felt trapped. She found herself taking frequent walks in the garden, even if the weather was unfavourable. But even then, she had little peace. Apparently, she wasn't the only one with that *plan*. The number of times Jasper sent Ocheridge out to her and staged their meeting to appear as a coincidence was really laughable.

The only meaningful communication she had with the Scotsman were the notes they began sending to each other.

Delivered secretly and pushed under bedroom doors, they could be opened in solitude after the rest of the house had gone to bed. She'd replied to the original monkey-groom with a tongue-in-cheek portrait of her potential simian in-laws, and a back-and-forth had begun. Writing a reply, or reading his, had become Beatrice's favourite part of the day.

She did manage to talk in person with Mr Mackenzie a little, though due to the observed nature of these conversations, the information she learnt was basic. He was born in Cromarty but didn't want to talk about his childhood. He liked horseback riding but not hunting. And he liked to read, though had a tendency to read a book in one sitting lest he forget and never finish it.

That wasn't a lot, but it gave her a better idea of the man he was. And even though he hadn't been able to say much, the *way* he said those things contained valuable information as well.

She could tell now when he was being genuinely kind as opposed to socially polite — his smile always reached his eyes when it was genuine niceness — and she could tell when he was holding himself back. Sometimes this would be a clenching of knuckles and a mouth set into a hard line. Other times there would be an unnatural pause — or trailing off — in the middle of a sentence that led her to believe he'd frequently been told nobody wanted to hear him. She'd lived with Jasper long enough to know how that made someone feel.

She couldn't help but be intrigued by him. The more Jasper tried to stop her from getting to know him, the more she wanted to learn.

She couldn't wait for Mrs Lutton's ball. Not only would it provide some much-needed levity to counter the tensions of Godshollow, but it would be an opportunity for Beatrice to spend time with Mr Mackenzie without the overbearing presence of Jasper. Jasper did *not* like balls. If ever he was forced to attend one, he spent his time in the card room, relying on Mrs Lutton's word that she was a good chaperone — even Jasper couldn't argue against the formidable woman. He'd left his sister in the older woman's care for the past few balls in area, and so far there had been no life-ruining scandals.

Beatrice's planning meetings with Mrs Lutton were a godsend. She was the only person Beatrice could talk to honestly about everything. She alone could understand her situation and feelings. Beatrice *had* been writing to Annabelle. But while she had fun discussing romantic fantasies, that wasn't quite what she needed. Mrs Lutton could provide a more grounded view of events.

"I'm glad to hear that, despite your brother's efforts, you've gotten to know the man a little better and find him agreeable. But tell me, dear, if he weren't here to come into possession of Godshollow, would you still pursue him?"

"I would." This revelation left her feeling as though she'd been kicked by a cart horse. Her pursuit of the man had nothing to do with the security of her future. She liked him not because he was simply a better alternative than Ocheridge, but because he was a nice man. Had his visit been nothing more than a simple visit to some neighbours, for example, they could have had a normal courtship. Perhaps Jasper would take some time to get over his disappointment for her rejection of Ocheridge, but he'd see she and Duncan could be happy together and not be driven by spite against the man who wanted to take their home.

"Thank goodness," Mrs Lutton replied cheerfully. "Now that you have made a connection with him, I can be honest with you." She put her teacup down on the side table and cleared her throat.

"You know I would never interfere with your decisions. Like me, I think, once your mind is made up, that is the end of it, and I applaud your determination to take care of your family, but . . . Well, frankly, my dear, marrying for perceived security was the worst decision I ever made."

"I did sense that you weren't overly enthusiastic about it. But thank you for respecting my decision. I don't think I'm out of danger yet. It's true that I like him, and he responds to me well, but I can't know definitely if he has any romantic feelings for me."

"If he doesn't, he's far more stupid than I gave him credit for. Though, if he doesn't, he will after this ball you've put so much effort into. I'll do everything I can to assist your budding courtship. It's a shame poor Annabelle is still on bed rest from having her baby. I'm sure she'd love all this romance."

"Indeed. She was already upset about missing the ball — she'll be even more so now. Although she has been sending me all kinds of advice, suggesting little scenes I might orchestrate to kindle affection. Most of them are wonderfully absurd, but one of them might work."

The afternoon before the ball, Beatrice finally had a chance to try one of Annabelle's suggestions.

She was sitting in the parlour. Because the day was bright and sunny, she opened the window, letting in the summery breeze and the sweet smell of a garden basking in the sun.

She was having a rare moment of time to herself. Jasper had left her a note saying he and Mr Mackenzie had gone into town, so she was quite happily sewing the last few decorative stitches to her headband for that evening when she heard a gentle tune drifting on the gentle breeze.

Bee-o, bee-o, bonnie bairn o mine.

It wasn't uncommon for the gardener to hum or whistle whilst going about his work, but this little ditty had a particularly Scottish lilt. With surprise, she looked out the window and saw Mr Mackenzie wandering between the bushes. Clearly Jasper had lied about their trip. Or at least, about Mr Mackenzie accompanying him.

This prompted her to make the decision that this was a lovely time for a walk. She'd always intended to go out into the garden anyway to pick some last-minute flowers—this just hastened the inevitable. If she happened to bump into Mr Mackenzie and have a nice conversation with him, then so be it. Jasper couldn't get mad if their meeting happened by accident.

So she grabbed her basket and her shears and headed out the back door. Mr Mackenzie had advanced in his walk. He was moving from the neat pink and yellow rows of posies and petunias that formed bright little guidelines for the walker to follow and was nearing the edge of the sculptured garden. Beyond that, large, untameable dahlia and rhododendron bushes supplied a blend to the trees and ancient woodland that expanded out across the countryside, the spots of red and blue giving way to a sea of greens.

She was going to have to cross the garden, and Annabelle had instructed that it was imperative she not seem to be following him. She wandered down the path, brushing her fingers along the lilacs and potentilla until she found some white roses at just the right stage of bloom for vase flowers, newly bloomed enough that they weren't going to decay before the ball even started, but not so new that their full bloom wouldn't be realised too late.

She looked up to observe Mr Mackenzie's progress and saw he'd changed his direction. Instead of continuing into the woodland, he was coming towards her. She smiled to herself happily.

She set her basket on the ground, took her shears, and leant towards the back of the rose bush. Her hand was outstretched, trying to grab a flower, and she was up on her tiptoes, one foot stuck out behind her. She felt slightly silly, audibly straining and making panicked noises, hoping Mr Mackenzie would see how precarious her situation was—if Jasper just let her talk to him like a normal person, she wouldn't have to come up with ridiculous ways to get him to talk to her that could be quickly explained as an accident should Jasper come across them. She felt even sillier however, when the acting became reality and she really was heading for a dive into the bush.

She flailed her arms as she tried to re-establish her balance, but her attempts to save herself were proving to be ineffectual. She covered her face to protect herself from the thorns and allowed gravity to drag her down, landing among the bramble of rose thorns and the dense foliage of the neighbouring bush.

She heard a shout of "Ach! Jesus" and then felt strong hands haul her out of the bush.

"I'm so sorry, lass." Mr Mackenzie brought her onto the path, holding her close. "I saw ye falling but I didnae get here in time. Are ye all right?"

Beatrice pushed her loose and tangled hair out of her eyes. That hadn't happened exactly as she'd imagined, but the result was very good.

"I'm fine," she replied. "Thank you for your help. I might have been stuck in there all night if you hadn't pulled me out."

Mr Mackenzie held her at arm's length. He ran his eyes over her body, then held her gaze. A shiver coursed through Beatrice's body. She felt as though he was looking into her soul.

He mistook her physical reaction for one of pain and began to gently press his fingers along her hair line, as if checking for injury.

"Just a wee scratch," he mentioned as he touched her right temple. "Ye should be more careful. Roses are beautiful, but they're nasty wee buggers under the petals."

"I know, it was silly. But I just wanted the best for the ball."

"Oh, aye?" he asked with a smile. He picked one of the roses from the basket, his thick leather gloves protecting him as he divested the stem of thorns. Then he brushed a few strands of her hair away from her forehead and plucked leaves and twigs out of it, placing the flower delicately behind her ear.

"While the leaves do match yer eyes, the white stands out against the ebony of yer hair." He laughed. "That, and I think flowers are more acceptable than the rest of the foliage."

A warm feeling spread through her core, tingling down to her toes. He'd been so gentle and observant. It never occurred to her that he would make time to notice the colour of her eyes or what colours showed her to her best advantage. She tried to stop her heart fluttering as though she was a schoolgirl and at the same time keep her composure.

"Thorns do make for uncomfortable headwear," Beatrice replied with a coy smile. "Though I think a *red* rose might suit *you* better. I take it you'll be wearing your kilt this evening."

Goodness, how badly she hoped he would wear his kilt again. That would fit perfectly with the evening she and Mrs Lutton had planned, but mostly she had to admit she just liked seeing him in it.

"Well," Mr Mackenzie said thoughtfully. "I could. But only if ye promise me the first two dances."

"I think I can agree to those conditions."

He chuckled and picked up Beatrice's basket. "I cannae wait tae see what ye've been planning. Ye've been very secretive." He held his arm out to Beatrice to escort her inside. She took it.

"That *is* the general premise of a surprise," she joked. "Tell me, did you attend a lot of balls in Scotland?"

Mr Mackenzie paused. "Nae really. I didnae have the opportunity."

"Well, I'm sure you'll enjoy it tonight. The longer you stay in England, the more you'll find that going to balls is a national pastime around here."

"Aye," he replied plainly. "It isnae so different in Scotland, I just wasnae a part of it."

"Well, hopefully you'll have a good time tonight to make up for it."

They'd reached the back door. He held it open for her then handed back her basket.

"We'll see," he replied promisingly as he followed her into the building. "I'd best start tae get ready. I wouldnae want tae disappoint."

Beatrice smiled. "Quite right. We mustn't be late. Mrs Lutton would never forgive us."

CHAPTER THIRTEEN

A pleat on Duncan's kilt refused to fold neatly. The right-hand fold bulged in the middle, going wider than the rest, creating a nasty, eye-catching bump to the side of the pleat. That wouldn't have been a problem if it was a side, or back pleat, but this one was front and centre, making his whole face-on profile wonky.

Nothing he was doing was helping and he was getting frustrated with it. He couldn't go to the ball looking as though he'd slept in his clothes. And he couldn't let Miss Hartley down. Whether she knew it or not, she'd given him such an excited look when she'd asked about his kilt. He didn't want to disappoint her by looking dishevelled and untidy.

He had to quickly squash that trail of thought. Thinking about being dishevelled in the presence of Miss Hartley would lead him to imaginings that were not befitting of a gentleman.

Instead, he turned his attention back to his stubborn pleat. He was fast running out of time, and he needed to fix it. He tried pressing the cloth under the heavy book he'd borrowed from the Godshollow library. He tried wetting it and reshaping it. He couldn't even hide the unsightly problem beneath his sporran.

He threw himself onto the bed out of stress, but soon jumped up quickly with a yelp as something stabbed into the back of his leg. He searched the sheets for the offending pricker and found his nanna's brooch lying in the folds. It must have fallen out of his bag the last time he put it on the bed.

He shouldn't have had it, really. The pin was supposed to pass down from mother to daughter, meaning *his* mother should have inherited when his nanna passed away. But the wise woman had entrusted her brooch to him. She'd always talked about how she hated the idea of all of her belongings being passed to her—in her own words—good-for-nothing son and his cold, heartless wife.

A few years before his nanna died, she'd been taken quite seriously ill. Thinking the end was near, Duncan's uncle and mother had begun to take an inventory of his nanna's belongings, looking for things that would bring them a lot of money.

Truthfully, the brooch probably wasn't worth that much, but when his mother had started eyeing it up, his nanna had decided it was her sincerest wish she never get her *grubby wee talons* on it.

Whilst the others had mourned her recovery, Duncan had been entrusted with the brooch, along with the silhouettes he'd set up the first night he spent at Godshollow.

The brooch wasn't fancy per se, small and quite plain, with a simple pattern worked into the silver cross. But it fit perfectly with his nanna's character, and Duncan realised it could perfectly solve his current problem.

He fixed it in place, tucking the unruly fold into the right position and securing it with the metal pin. Using his small hand mirror, he checked how it looked, and finding it smart and not garish, he was satisfied.

Feeling much more comfortable, and bolstered by the remembrance of his nanna, Duncan made his way to the entry hall to meet with Miss Hartley and Mr Ocheridge, who had insisted on inviting himself and going with them from Godshollow.

Only the gentleman—if he could really be described so— was waiting when Duncan arrived at the meeting point. Miss

Hartley had yet to descend.

He gave Mr Ocheridge a polite nod and was completely happy to wait in silence for the last of their party to arrive. Mr Ocheridge, it seemed, wasn't.

"That's a very *interesting* choice of apparel," he commented snottily. "Around here, it's polite to wear strictly formal attire for a ball."

"Aye, this *is* formal," he answered shortly. "This is the most formal ye can get in Scotland."

Ocheridge sniffed and placed his hand on his chest. "Of course, *I'm* not saying it doesn't look formal. I'm just saying that *others* may see it that way. I only wanted to prepare you for standing the odd looks you may receive. *I* think it looks marvellous, of course, but I'm not everybody."

Duncan sighed quietly. He supposed Ocheridge was expecting to be thanked for his *service,* but luckily he didn't have to supply any retort, because they were interrupted by the arrival of Miss Hartley and he was struck dumb.

The radiance of Miss Hartley had driven all logical and reasonable thoughts from his mind. She was wearing a deep blue gown with cream coloured edge trimmings, a warm colour that hugged his eyes as much as it hugged *her* figure.

Her brilliant black hair was neatly curled and pinned, and nestled amid the ebony coils was a white rose from the garden. Duncan hadn't noticed it at first, but when she turned her head, it shone like a beacon.

Could he be so presumptuous to think she'd put it in her hair for him? That seemed too specific to be a coincidence. It could only be a result of their moment in the garden.

He hadn't been lying or using empty flattery when he told her the colour suited her. The flower did everything he said and more. She was beautiful. He was finding his feelings hard to actually put into words.

For the time being, he could only stand there with his

mouth agape as he fought to find words good enough to do her justice.

Mr Ocheridge, as usual, couldn't keep his mouth shut. He pushed past Duncan to get to Miss Hartley. Standing beside her, the lawyer looked awful—pallid, thin, and stooped, a man who spent all of his time indoors, hunched over a desk, not outside in the sun—a masquerade mask would significantly improve his looks when they donned them at the venue. Miss Hartley seemed just as repulsed by him as Duncan was, if her manner when he kissed her hand was any indication.

Duncan wanted to gloat when she released Ocheridge and came to him. She looked up at him, tilting her face so she was gazing through her lashes rather than having direct eye contact. She daintily draped her gloved hand over his forearm.

She was utterly gorgeous.

"Mr Mackenzie, would you be so kind as to escort me to the carriage?"

When Duncan was little, his nanna had read him stories, and he always laughed at the sailors who were tempted by beauty and met their downfall at the hands of the Korrigan. Now, he could completely understand the bewitching effect of the right woman.

He was called back to his senses by Ocheridge's obsequiousness.

"I'd happily escort you, Miss Hartley. It seems Mr Mackenzie isn't feeling up to it."

"Thank ye fer yer concern, but I'm quite fine. Are you ready, Miss Hartley?"

"Very. Mr Ocheridge, perhaps you might get the door?"

The lawyer was obviously annoyed that he'd been passed over in favour of Duncan, but chose to remain silent.

Duncan was chagrined, however, when Ocheridge took his revenge. As Duncan held the carriage door for Miss Hartley,

Ocheridge quickly followed her inside, closing the door in Duncan's face—it was clear he wasn't welcome inside. He could have wrestled with Ocheridge to open the door, as he knew he was stronger, but he also knew there would be time enough at the ball for him to gain Miss Hartley's attention.

He found himself relegated to the seat next to the driver, whilst Ocheridge had Miss Hartley to himself, warm inside the carriage.

The driver was a poor substitute for Miss Hartley. He was a balding old man who coughed and sniffed and yelled obscenities at the horses. Duncan tried to put as big a space between them as he could.

When they arrived at Havenbrooke Hall, Duncan could only follow the pair into the venue as they continued a conversation that had been started on the journey.

"But who will be counting if we dance more than two together?"

"Believe me, Mr Ocheridge, society mothers are the greatest gossips in the country. However, much as it would be *nice* to dance more than two with a partner, I am only worried about *your* reputation. You are a masterful lawyer, but idle gossip has felled many men. A poor reputation is infinitely more long-lasting than a moment of pleasure."

That crafty vixen. She was a master of the backhanded compliment and the distracting appeal to a man's pride. These tactics only worked on men like Ocheridge who believed they were the source of sunshine on the earth, but never had Duncan seen them used with such finesse.

"Oh, yes. I suppose you're right. I know that Mr Favering had a dalliance with his maidservant, and the gossip closed down his medical practice."

"Indeed. Of course, you are *much* more well-established and better respected than he is, but the threat is no less real.

There will no doubt be wives of your business rivals who will seize upon any piece of intrigue they can."

Ocheridge was nodding his head like an enthusiastic puppy, completely oblivious to Miss Hartley's machinations. "You are so smart. Of course! Danderell has had it out for me from day one. I wonder if it would be wise for me to dance at all, to tell you the truth."

Miss Hartley's head lifted a little and her shoulders rolled back. "I understand. I would be disappointed not to dance with you, but your career and reputation are much more important than my silly old feelings."

That was it, the final jab.

"You are most kind, Miss Hartley. Thank you for excusing me. Perhaps, when the guests start to leave later, we might have one dance together."

"If the fates allow, Mr Ocheridge."

And then the fool left for the card rooms, leaving them in the entrance hall. Duncan almost felt sorry for Ocheridge, Miss Hartley had easily manipulated him into leaving her alone. The sympathy was only fleeting.

A beaming Mrs Lutton approached them. She greeted Miss Hartley with an affectionate hug and Duncan with a clasping of hands.

"I'm so glad you could make it, Mr Mackenzie. Tell me, what do you think of our theme?"

Duncan took a moment to really look at the decorations in the ballroom, having paid them no attention before. He found himself speechless.

This was unlike anything he'd seen before. Every surface was draped in blue taffeta or brightly patterned tartan. Blue and white streamers hung from the ceiling, and hundreds of vases filled with blue forget-me-nots, white roses, and purple thistles lined the room.

The decoration that really caught his eye was the large

Scottish flag that hung from the bannister of the main stair-case, leaving no doubt as to what had inspired the theme of this ball.

Miss Hartley turned to face him cautiously, her voice apprehensive.

"Do you like it?"

That was a simple question, but Duncan couldn't find a way to express his opinion. A tumult of emotion coursed through him that he couldn't explain to himself, let alone anyone else. His stomach was a battleground for competing nerves, excitement, and horrid remembrance.

In his family, Scottish pride was paramount, but where his nanna had brought him up to be proud of his nationality, his uncle had used it against him.

"Ye'll never be a true Scotsman. Ye may live here, but ye havenae the heart. Yer a disgrace tae this family."

Of course, Duncan always tried to remember his nanna's word, not his uncle's. But the older man's sustained campaign of insults had taken their toll.

A lump formed in his throat, preventing him from giving an answer. Unfortunately, Miss Hartley took his silence as disapproval rather than emotion.

"Is something wrong, Mr Mackenzie? Don't say I've gone to all this trouble and failed to make this ball even remotely Scottish." He knew she was joking, trying to cut through the tension, but Duncan could sense she really was concerned she'd offended him. He swallowed his anxiety as best he could and focussed on the positive aspects of the situation.

"Ye didnae fail, lass. I'd wager this ball is more Scottish than a ball *in* Scotland."

Miss Hartley's features relaxed into a relieved grin. "Thank goodness. I don't want to brag, but I'm very proud of my work. I would have hated to make a fool of myself."

"Ye've done a perfect job. Ye havenae missed a thing. Ye've got the colours, the flag, the thistles. And if I amnae mistaken

I think I can hear some of Robert Burns's poetry being re-cited."

"It is!" she replied excitedly. "General Lutton adores Burn's work and wanted to greet guests with it as they arrived." She pointed to the older gentleman across the room by the entrance to the ballroom who sat in a chair, book in hand, happily reciting as people mingled around him.

"I'm so glad you like it," she continued "We wanted to celebrate Godshollow's Scottish origins."

"That's very kind of ye, lass, though ye didnae have tae go tae all this trouble fer me."

Her smile widened and she batted him playfully on the arm. "Don't be ridiculous. Planning all this was thoroughly enjoyable. The more I learn about Gaelic culture, the more I love it. There's a very romantic feel to it, don't you think?"

There certainly was, and Duncan had an idea of how to encourage the romantic feeling . . . maybe even develop it into something more. "Ye've clearly done yer research. Tell me, what do ye know about the thistle?" He led her to a doorway where a thistle hung down from the head of the frame.

"Oh, plenty," she answered enthusiastically. "The thistle is a national symbol for the Scottish. Nobody really knows how it started, but there's a story that the Scots were saved from an invasion when one of the would-be invaders stood on a thistle and yelped in pain, alerting nearby Scots of the party's movements and enabling them to ambush the warriors and save their land. It became particularly important when James II created the Order of the Thistle in 1687."

Duncan was momentarily stunned. He'd expected an assertion that she'd found thistles to be a common symbol in Scotland, but she sounded ready to write a textbook on the subject.

"Very thorough," he praised. Now it was time to put his plan into action. "Though ye seem tae have forgotten a very important tradition."

"Oh, have I?"

"Aye. And it's very bad manners tae ignore it."

The corner of her mouth quirked into a smile. "And what might this tradition be?"

"Ye'll like it, I'm sure. Ye see, it's honoured tradition that if a gentleman finds himself under a doorway with a young lass and there's a thistle hanging above them, he has tae give her a kiss."

Her eyes went from concerned about a gap in her knowledge to a knowing gleam.

"Is that so? Just like mistletoe. That was a *severe* lapse in my research."

"I willnae hold it against ye."

"You're very kind."

He leant his head forwards slowly. "That is, only if ye remedy this *grievous* oversight by fulfilling the tradition."

She agreed with a twinkling laugh and mirrored his movements, ready to receive a kiss.

He wanted more than a gentle kiss on the cheek, but following mistletoe etiquette, he had to be content with the disappointment in Miss Hartley's eyes as she had also clearly expected more. A small peck on her right cheek was going to have to satisfy them.

Not that they had much time to dwell on it. Mrs Lutton soon whisked them away to be admired as the mastermind of the theme — Miss Hartley — and the inspiration for it — Duncan.

He soon found himself at the centre of a swarm of guests, half of whom were watching him as though he was a performing monkey, the other half eyeing him up like a joint of meat at the butcher's, pushing their young daughters forwards, masks snatched away to show off their beauty. He didn't know what they'd heard about him, but inhabitants of a quiet area like this were always going to get excitable about a new person.

Grateful when the time came to begin dancing, he was able to avoid the gaggle thanks to being committed to Miss Hartley for the first two dances.

Not that that was the only reason for his being happy.

If he had to be honest, Duncan would have to say that the dancing was enjoyable. Miss Hartley was an enthusiastic partner and was determined to have fun, though she did have something to say before they started dancing.

"I hope I'm not denying you the happiness of dancing with one of those other young ladies," she ventured to say as they walked to the floor and took their place at the top of the set amongst some odd companions, such as a lion and his lioness, a jester and a princess, and many other wonderful masked characters.

"I have nae desire tae dance with anyone else," he said honestly.

"You're sure? You wouldn't rather sample the best that English society has to offer?" Miss Hartley teasingly remarked.

"You speak as though the ladies here are like cattle, tae be paraded fer a farmer," he countered.

"Are we not? Women's lives are dedicated to finding and keeping a husband. We spend our time showing men our worthiness as a wife, just as a farmer would seek to show a heifer's milk production or fertility. And if you are given Godshollow, as I'm sure you will be, it will need a mistress."

"That may be the case, but I'm nae in the market for a heifer."

"*You* may not be," she replied with a smirk. "But *they* certainly are in the market for a gentleman. And you're the first new face they've seen in a long time. Though . . . it's not so much them you need to be wary of, but their mothers." As if to illustrate Miss Hartley's point, an eager *mama* gave him a coy wave and a wink as she walked past them to get to the benches.

Whatever romantic tension had been building during the conversation soon gave way to laughter as neither could resist the comedy of the moment.

And the jollies continued as the dance began. As Duncan watched her throw herself bodily into the quadrille, he could readily imagine her as the person who might be able to bring love back into his life. She was kind and fun, and she allowed him to release his anger and upset. The more she pulled Duncan into her world, the more he let go of his negative feelings, letting his bitterness wash away on the swell of the music.

But as seemed Duncan's lot in life, the happiness couldn't last all night. After finishing a quadrille, Miss Hartley wished to have a drink. Duncan offered to fetch it for her. She declined, wanting to take the opportunity to leave the stuffy ballroom for a moment. He offered to go with her. She accepted. But as they made their way to the edge of the dancing space and into the crowd, a woman intercepted them.

"Mr Mackenzie," she greeted him as they drew closer. "Mrs Lutton said you're an actual Scot. You see, my friends and I are having a *wee* argument about something Scottish in nature. Would you please settle it for us?"

Duncan really wished he could say no, but the woman quickly took his arm and pulled him towards six people, two of whom were in the depths of a heated row.

The gentlemen stood in the hallway, talking at a volume high enough to draw a number of odd looks. As they drew closer, Duncan realised with dread that this was the group the lady wanted him to mediate.

"My god, Pollett," one red-faced man spat at the other. "When you lost your eye, was it a long time before they could close the hole to stop anything else leaking out?"

"Just what are you insinuating, Dodgerson?" retorted the eye-patched gentleman defensively.

"I'm merely suggesting that a good deal of your sense may have fallen into the sea that day at Trafalgar."

The lady who'd asked Duncan for his assistance tutted like a school mistress. "Now, now you two, stop arguing. I have brought an answer to your debate. Mr Mackenzie, if you could, please . . ." She gestured for Duncan to *take the floor*.

"Aye," he agreed apprehensively. "What seems tae be yer question?"

"Well," said the red man, pushing the other aside. "Pollett here was trying to argue that haggis was for eating. But it sounds ghastly! He has to be joking."

Duncan tried to diplomatically settle the dispute, but the men just kept asking question after question, cutting each other off and talking over Duncan before he could even answer.

"Do you have to live in a certain place to be a Highlander?"

"Aye, it's – "

"What kind of importance does a stone have to the law of rule? And why is it named after the little cakes?"

"It isnae – "

"Things must be so much better now that Scotland is under British rule. Why on earth are people still complaining about it?"

This last question had caused another violent shouting match between the two men, and Duncan used that as his opportunity to escape.

Stepping away from the group, Duncan scanned the crowd for Miss Hartley. He searched for the raven hair and the deep blue gown, but she was perfectly suited to the theme, making her impossible to find.

In the end, he decided he needed some air. He could come back and look for Miss Hartley once he wasn't feeling so claustrophobic. He stopped to have a quiet word with Mrs Lutton.

"Have ye anywhere I can go fer a wee bit of air and peace? Somewhere others wouldnae likely use."

With a twinkle in her eye, the hostess directed Duncan to an outside balcony on the far east side of the manor, past the ballroom into the dining areas where the building was split into two floors. There were several balconies, most of which seemed to be in use. But Mrs Lutton took him farther back to a spot where the music and guests were minimal — this was the benefit of asking the hostess; she would know the areas that people were less likely to visit. It was perfect, and given the size of the place, Duncan was sure he would have never found it on his own.

The small cosy outside area was wonderfully quiet when the door was shut, and the view was pleasantly calming. The balcony looked out over a pristine garden set in bright rows of colourful flowers, creating a floral border around a magnificent stone fountain, which was in itself very peaceful. A life-sized stone woman was pouring water from her amphora into the pond below in a gentle, steady flow.

Duncan felt relieved to be out of the oppressive noise, heat, and yes, Scottishness, of the dance room and the busy hall in general. Though he couldn't help but feel lonely, a feeling he was accustomed to, but one which seemed amplified in that moment.

"Is there room for one more out there with you?"

Duncan turned to see Miss Hartley standing in the doorway, letting the cool night air flow into the stuffy house. He nodded and shut the door behind her as she joined him. She stood mere inches from him, even though there was no lack of room.

"Are ye enjoying the party?" he asked conversationally, trying to ignore being close enough to see the different shades that went into her beautiful green eyes.

"I'm worried that you're not," she replied slowly.

"That's kind of ye, lass, but ye dunnae need tae worry about me. I just came out tae get some air."

She went quiet for a moment. Then she looked up at him, her eyes watching him from beneath her lashes.

"I never meant to upset you with this theme," she admitted.

"I didnae say ye did."

"But you're clearly unhappy about it. Your face when you first came in, you went pale." She really was a straightforward woman.

Duncan didn't answer.

Miss Hartley sighed and faced him, hands on hips. "I like you Mr Mackenzie" — she was *incredibly* forward — "and I'm trying to get to know more about you, but I feel as though you're shutting me out. I hardly know anything about you. Why don't you want me to?"

Panic hit him like a punch to the stomach.

"I . . . I like ye too, lass . . . I dunnae . . . I didnae . . . I—"

"I know we haven't really known each other very long. I understand not wanting to share personal information with strangers." She paused and played with the lace on the frill of her cuff. "But you have to admit we're more than strangers."

The look in her eyes was heartbreakingly hopeful.

"Aye, lass," he said gently. "I'd say we were."

"Then talk to me," she implored. "You look like you're carrying the weight of the world on your shoulders and need a good friend to talk to."

A small hand gently brushed hair away from his temple and came to rest on his bicep.

"I'm not going to tell anyone anything you say, if that's what you're worried about. Even in such a short time, you must have noticed my brother and I have a strained relationship."

"It isnae that . . . I cannae . . . I dunnae . . ." He paused and let out a breath. "Ye dunnae want tae worry about ma problems, lass."

To his astonishment, she reached up onto her toes, using his shoulder to steady herself, drawing level with his ear.

"That's for me to decide, isn't it?"

Her warm breath tickled the skin of his neck as she spoke, leaving him feeling ice cold when she moved away. He was stunned into silence.

That apparently wasn't what Miss Hartley wanted, because she soon filled the air between them with sound. "You need to talk to someone. You need someone to trust."

He thought of his nanna. She'd been that person his entire life, and he missed the warmth they shared. "I had someone," he muttered spitefully. "But she just proved tae me that ye cannae trust anyone."

"She must have been very special to you," Miss Hartley commented, dropping back down in poorly hidden disappointment. "Is she back in Scotland?"

"Aye, she was special," Duncan replied wearily. "But in the end, she left me, just like everyone else."

"Did she choose another?"

"Nae." He drew a breath, trying to steady his voice. "She died. She wasnae old, she wasnae ill, but one day I came tae wake her, and she'd gone."

"I'm so sorry," Miss Hartley offered. "What was her name?"

Duncan laughed. "Caitlín. Though she hated it. She wanted everyone tae call her Cait. She didn't like formality. I was always tae call her nanna, never grandmother."

Miss Hartley blinked. "Oh. This woman was your grandmother?"

"Ye sound a wee bit relieved, Miss Hartley. Dare I ask who ye thought I was talking about?"

"Nobody in particular," she was quick to assure him,

though unconvincingly. "I may have assumed it was someone else, but you said she wasn't old."

"Well, she was only sixty," Duncan countered. "Her mother lived tae ninety-seven. Compared tae that, sixty is nae very old."

"It very much isn't," she replied. "Is it because of her you're here now?"

And somehow Duncan found himself explaining everything.

"Aye. With ma nanna gone, I didnae have a reason tae stay in Scotland. She brought me up on tales of Godshollow, so I thought it would be a good place tae restart ma life."

"Why couldn't you stay in Scotland?"

"Ma uncle," he told her. "Ma father died when I was a wee lad. Ma mother married ma uncle, and he became ma guardian. He was tae look after ma inheritance until I came of age.

"He hated me and made ma life miserable. He was a good manipulator. He turned ma own mother against me along with most of our neighbours by spreading lies. He even turned me against maself, convinced me I was worthless and a nuisance. But ma nanna loved me and took care of me.

"She commanded a lot of respect in the town and people didnae like tae oppose her. She tried tae stop as much of ma abuse as possible. Once she died though, I knew ma treatment would only get worse. Graeme had nae intention of honouring ma inheritance. It turned out over the years he'd used his power over ma estate tae give most of it tae himself. He left me with nothing. I was nae longer welcome in ma own home."

He grew more and more worried with every second Miss Hartley remained quiet.

"Damn," she said. "That's a heart-breakingly legitimate reason. I feel so selfish now.

Acting on pure feeling, Duncan laughed, loud and long

and clear, and then leant forwards and pressed his lips against hers, as though a dam had broken and he couldn't hold back his desire any longer.

If Miss Hartley was surprised, she didn't show it. She didn't push him away or shout at him for his impropriety. Something told Duncan that she needed this kiss as much as he did.

They finally broke apart, gasping for air. His heart was racing, her face was flushed.

"I'm so sorry, lass. I didnae mean it tae happen like that."

"But you did intend it to happen?"

His eyes went wide. "Oh Laird, ye must think me an utter fool!"

She held up a hand to stop him. "Did I say I was cross?"

CHAPTER FOURTEEN

Beatrice's whole body tingled. She never would have predicted how this evening would go. She'd expected she would experience more emotion than usual, but this was so much more than she could have imagined.

When she'd asked Mr Mackenzie to talk to her, to tell her things, she'd expected his usual attempts to avoid conversation. Somehow she'd managed to convince him to open up, which had culminated in that heated kiss.

From his behaviour, she'd always suspected his life hadn't been an easy one. With what he'd told her, she could understand why he kept that to himself. Most people wouldn't have been able to live through such a tragedy—she greatly admired his strength.

And of course, she was now sorry that she'd ever hoped he wouldn't get Godshollow.

She was quite certain she could have stayed out there all night, talking with him, receiving another few kisses, if they were available. Fortunately, Mrs Lutton had arrived to let them know they'd been away for so long that people would soon notice their joint absence.

The ball went on another two hours after their meeting on the balcony, though they didn't get to spend much more time together. Mr Mackenzie was called away by Mrs Lutton to be introduced to several families. Beatrice was engaged by an acquaintance from town, Phillipa Morton, who loved to talk and hated to listen.

At one o'clock, the ball was considered over, most of the

guests having left. Mr Ocheridge met Beatrice and Mr Mackenzie to wait for the carriage, grumpy and uncooperative, having lost a significant amount on cards. He was very put out to learn Mr Mackenzie had danced with Beatrice.

And that wasn't his only complaint of the evening. Ocheridge spent the journey back to Godshollow expressing every single thought he had about the ball, down to the smallest minutiae of the decorations. For example, how the whiskey glass was an inferior make to his own, as it had far too narrow a base for swirling properly, or so he said.

But as they drew closer to Godshollow, his demeanour changed. He was constantly fidgeting, feet tapping, fingers wiggling, eyes darting. Beatrice was growing nervous just watching him.

In the end, it seemed his anxiety was perfectly appropriate. When they reached Godshollow, they found a scene of utter chaos.

The whole world and his wife appeared to be gathered in the courtyard with lamps and torches. The clamour was so loud as to spook the horses, meaning the party had to stop outside the gates and walk.

Beatrice tried to push her way through the crowd, Mr Mackenzie close behind her, a protective hand placed on the small of her back. But surprisingly, it was Mr Ocheridge who managed to get them to the epicentre of the congregation. With a command and authority Beatrice could never have imagined he possessed, he drove a path through the crowd.

In the centre, they found Jasper, furious and shocked, shouting loudly at the local magistrate who was trying to calm him down, and Mr Peters, looking as though he'd much rather have been in bed.

The steward tried to stop them from going any farther.

"Stay back, Miss," he instructed.

"But what's going on?"

The answer wasn't long in coming. When Jasper saw Mr Mackenzie, his shouting became even more hysterical.

"It was him," he cried, pointing to the bewildered Mr Mackenzie. "Arrest him! You won't get away with this, you filthy cur."

"Jasper," Beatrice cried. "What's happened?" She had a momentary panic and feared word had reached Jasper somehow of her and Mr Mackenzie's kiss on the balcony.

Jasper was apoplectic with rage "He broke into my study." He pointed to the side of the castle. The light from the crowd's lamps shone upon a dreadful scene.

"I wasnae anywhere near yer office. I havenae done anything."

A large hole gaped like a wound in the window of Jasper's ground floor study. Somebody had clearly broken in. Beatrice walked closer and peered inside. Furniture had been thrown, papers were scattered everywhere, and broken glass covered the carpet in front of the window. A furious search had obviously taken place, though Beatrice couldn't understand for a moment what Jasper might have that he thought Mr Mackenzie would want to steal.

"When did this happen?" she asked in bewilderment.

"We think it was done during the ball, sometime within the last few hours, when Major Hartley was taking a constitutional before bed." Mr Peters explained.

"Then it cannae be me," Mr Mackenzie asserted. "I was at Havenbrooke the entire evening."

Beatrice nodded. "The whole night," she agreed.

"Then why did I find a piece of tartan left on the glass?" Jasper waved a piece of material like it was a smoking gun.

"That cannae be mine!" Mr Mackenzie asserted.

"Nice try. But it matches your kilt," Jasper replied, handing the material to the magistrate. "You see."

The magistrate held the material close to Mr Mackenzie's

hip to compare the fabrics. "I concur that this piece is of the same material as the kilt," he said at length.

This caused a flurry of chatter amongst the crowd.

"I dunnae have any fabric missing," Mr Mackenzie defended.

"I can't see any holes," Beatrice added. "And the whole of Havenbrooke Hall was decorated with tartan this evening. It could have come from anywhere." It was utterly impossible that Mr Mackenzie had committed this crime, so why was Jasper so insistent that he had?

"Why is the front pinned?" the magistrate asked calmly.

Beatrice hadn't noticed that. Even so, the brooch could have been there for any number of reasons.

"It wouldnae lie flat. Look, I didnae break intae that study!" Mr Mackenzie repeated. "Why would I?"

"I checked my papers." Jasper put in. "All that was missing was your heritage documents and Mr Daniels's address from my book."

Mr Mackenzie was stunned. "Ye've lost ma papers?" he asked slowly, as though he was trying to comprehend the words as he spoke them.

Jasper didn't even bother to acknowledge the question. Beatrice felt she had to step in.

"Why would Mr Mackenzie steal his own papers? He knows you've sent the letter to Mr Daniels. Why would he feel the need to contact him?" Nothing was adding up, though Jasper seemed desperate to have it so. "And also, why would he break in from the outside? It would have been much easier for him to break the lock on the door."

Jasper wasn't happy.

"He did it, I tell you," he screamed furiously. "The tartan proves it. Do something."

"You can't arrest him," Beatrice cried.

"Will you stop putting your nose in where it isn't wanted?"

Jasper bellowed at her. "You silly little girl."

"But he didn't do it. He was at the ball all night. I promise you."

The magistrate held up a hand. "You were with him at all times?"

"Not *every* moment, but—"

Mr Ocheridge chose this as his moment to join the argument.

"He was absent from the ball, though, for a considerable amount of time, an hour or more, so I was told. I heard Miss Morton mention it to her father who was playing cards with me at the time. She had been hoping of a dance with Mr Mackenzie, heaven knows why, but she was disappointed when she couldn't find him."

"That isnae enough time tae do anything," Mr Mackenzie argued.

"But it is," Ocheridge responded smugly. "There were plenty of carriages and horses in the courtyard at Havenbrooke. At full gallop, you could get to Godshollow in under twenty minutes, with the same time to get back, you had more than enough time to ransack that room."

"I didnae leave Havenbrooke."

"But nobody saw you. Where were you?"

Beatrice was presented with a problem. She could tell Jasper and everyone listening where Mr Mackenzie had been, and with whom. This would ruin her reputation. On the other hand, if she didn't speak up Mr Mackenzie would be falsely imprisoned. The choice was clear.

"That's ridiculous," she replied, but Mr Mackenzie stopped her from saying anything else.

"Mr Peters," he said, cutting across her. "I think ye might want tae take Miss Hartley inside. This isnae a place fer a lady."

"But—" She tried again to make her speech.

"I willnae have ye lie fer me, lass," Mr Mackenzie said loudly. What was he doing?

"It's not a lie!"

Mr Mackenzie turned his back on the men and turned to talk to just her. In a low voice he tried to explain.

"I willnae have ye losing yer reputation fer me. A young lady alone with a man who isnae her fiancé is asking fer trouble."

"I don't care."

"I do."

"No."

"Please, lass. It's clear I havenae done anything. Ye dunnae need tae risk yer future."

Beatrice bit her lip. Were there other arguments she could try first?

She stepped past Mr Mackenzie and back to her brother, but Jasper spoke before she could.

"Why are we standing around waiting for him to come up with excuses and lies? Arrest him already!" He moved forwards and grabbed Mr Mackenzie's arm, trying to pull him to the magistrate's carriage.

The magistrate, however, got in the way, separating the two men with a firm hand on Jasper's arm.

"This won't be solved tonight," he stated authoritatively. "Mr Mackenzie, you will accompany me to the gaol. You can stay there until we can view the evidence properly and see if anyone can come forward and claim where you were."

Beatrice's stomach dropped.

"No," she repeated. "You can't take him. This is ludicrous. Jasper, stop this."

When a struggle ensued, Beatrice tried to get in between the magistrate and Mr Mackenzie. Jasper tried to get her *out* of the way. She was pushed. She had no way of knowing for sure, but she was fairly certain Jasper's hands that had propelled her. Slipping, she fell against the outer wall of the castle and banged her head against the stone.

Chaos ensued.

Angry shouting rose and intensified as Jasper and Mr Mackenzie accused each other of pushing her.

Dazed, and with her head throbbing, Beatrice continued to protest Mr Mackenzie's innocence, but no one was listening to her. Mr Peters soon bustled her inside to check her head.

"This nasty break-in business will be sorted, Miss," he assured her. "Don't you worry. The truth will out. There's nothing more can be done tonight."

But Beatrice wouldn't be calmed. She tried to go back out to help Mr Mackenzie, but Mr Peters physically held her back. Her headache worsened as well, and eventually she allowed her maid to take her to bed, along with a tincture from the medicine chest to help her sleep.

She woke in the morning to voices outside her bedroom door. Jasper and Mr Ocheridge were deep in conversation. They were attempting to use hushed tones, but failing miserably, and their apparent excitement made them perfectly audible to Beatrice.

"It's quite possible then that she might have lost her memory?" Mr Ocheridge sounded hopeful.

"I've seen it happen," Jasper replied tentatively. "I've watched good men forget their own names after a simple knock to the head."

"It would be fortunate if that did happen. It would certainly help us if she thought the Scotsman at fault. We're running out of time, I fear. And *you* are running out of money. I know you have debtors chasing you. You can't afford for our plan to fail." Ocheridge's tone was threatening.

Beatrice's heart ached. Everything came down to money when Jasper was involved. What plan was Mr Ocheridge talking about? Something that involved herself and Mr Mackenzie. A horrible feeling rose from the pit of her stomach. Jasper and Ocheridge had staged the break-in. That was why nothing made sense—clearly anyone with a modicum of intelligence could see that Mr Mackenzie was innocent.

But why? The false arrest of Mr Mackenzie seemed far too drastic a step if they were only trying to stop him from getting Godshollow. They'd been acting so calmly, she'd assumed they expected the claim to fail. So what had changed? Having Mr Mackenzie incarcerated wouldn't stop Jasper's debtors, would it?

They both hoped for her injury to trouble her mind and clear it of what had happened. Jasper was right—she'd seen that happen before too. When she was a child, her friend William had been hit in the head with a cricket ball. For months afterwards he struggled to remember anything that had happened some three weeks before the accident. Eventually the memories returned, but that had been scary at the time.

If Beatrice wanted to find out what Jasper and Mr Ocheridge were planning, she needed to lull them into false security and make them believe their hopes had come to pass. She needed to pretend she couldn't remember anything.

Jasper was speaking again.

"Here's the doctor. He'll be able to tell us how bad she is."

The door to her room opened. They must have assumed she was still asleep, because they didn't knock.

"Miss Hartley?" Doctor Allen's was the first face she saw when she opened her eyes. It was his hand that had given her shoulder a gentle shake. She looked past him and saw Jasper watching with anticipation. Mr Ocheridge stood in the doorway. "I'm sorry I couldn't get here sooner. There was a very tricky birth I needed to tend to."

Beatrice didn't say anything. She had to maintain an illusion of fresh waking as Dr Allen helped her into a sitting position.

"How are you feeling?"

Beatrice took a few moments to answer, though she didn't have to lie. "It hurts."

The doctor ran his fingers lightly over her scalp. When he came across the bump on the back of her head, she groaned loudly.

Dr Allen let out a huff of breath. "That'll be the offender. Now, Miss Hartley, can you tell me how you hit your head?"

"I fell," she answered. She made her voice small and uncertain. She was interested in what explanation Jasper would offer in her stead.

"She was shoved," he related. "That hulking, brutish Scot pushed her, she fell backwards, and she hit her head on the wall."

"I *was* hoping Miss Hartley would answer for herself," the doctor said pointedly. "Does that match what you remember, Miss Hartley?"

She nearly laughed and destroyed her ruse. So that was the way he was going to distort the truth. She shook her head in a most sheepish fashion and cast a needful look towards Jasper.

Playing the *caring* brother, he came and knelt at her side. He took one of her hands in his. "You poor thing," he wheedled. "It was probably such a shock that your mind doesn't want to remember what happened."

He tutted and turned to Dr Allen. "My sister has been under stress recently. This Scot I was speaking of, he wanted to kidnap my sister and elope with her. He wanted to get back at me for proving he would never get possession of Godshollow, so he took something of mine. It's doubly awful, as she is already engaged to another."

"I'm engaged." She phrased it like a remembrance, though it begged to be a sardonic question, brimming with incredulity. Jasper was spinning this elaborate story that didn't even resemble the truth, and he clearly thought he could get away with it.

"That's right, dear," he encouraged. "To Mr Ocheridge, remember?"

Beatrice felt sick. Even in such a vulnerable state as he believed her to be in, he was pushing her to Ocheridge. Revealing her state of *compos mentis* was going to be a sweet victory in due time. For now, she just wanted to bring this conversation to an end.

"My head hurts," she mumbled pitifully, clutching her sore spot for emphasis.

Dr Allen searched through his bag. At length, he brought out a medicine bottle. "This should help." He poured the brown liquid onto a spoon and held it before Beatrice.

The medicine tasted awful. Someone had taken efforts to make it more palatable by adding some sugar, but the sweetness didn't help.

She forced herself to swallow.

"The pain will go away," Dr Allen was telling her. "If it comes back, you can take another dose. The memory loss is usual. Everything will probably come back to you in a few days."

"But it might not?" Jasper had every right to be nervous. When she *got her memories back*, she was not going to be easy on him.

Dr Allen pinched the bridge of his nose. "It's best to stay positive," he advised. "I'd say that if she can remember my visit tomorrow, she'll likely regain her other memories in time."

"Of course, of course," Jasper backtracked. "I just want her to be prepared for every eventuality."

The doctor hummed in uncertain agreement and packed up his bag. Before he left, he made sure to remind them to contact him if she got any worse.

Once he was gone, Jasper came to her bedside. He awkwardly tried to fluff her pillow and patted her hand.

"Now, don't you worry about a thing," he said condescendingly. "Mr Mackenzie has been properly detained. You don't need to worry about him anymore." He patted her shoulder and rose to his feet.

"Now, once you're feeling a little better, we can continue with the wedding planning, hmm?"

She nodded weakly, as inside a fire of disdain began to roar into life.

CHAPTER FIFTEEN

Duncan paced.

There wasn't particularly much else he could do, being trapped in a small, stone room. Thick metal rods in the windows stood between him and the outside, letting in some much-appreciated fresh air, but refusing him freedom.

The gaol was a surprisingly large building for the size of the town, with two wings to house criminals, separated by the gaoler's office. It had contained three doors. One for each wing, and one to enter the building.

The magistrate had escorted Duncan in and handed him over to the gaoler, giving a brief description of the charges. The gaoler then explained to Duncan that he would be kept in the gaol until such time as the crimes were heard before the court, or the magistrate's investigation proved his innocence.

When the magistrate left, Duncan was shown to his cell and left.

He couldn't sleep, so he paced. All he could do was to wait for the magistrate to return.

There weren't even any other jailed men for him to talk to. At about four o'clock in the morning, a butcher was brought in, arrested for drunken shenanigans. The man wasn't much company, sitting in the cell propped against the wall and snoring. So Duncan was indifferent to the appearance of the butcher's wife a little after five o'clock to take her husband home. Duncan was certain that staying a while in the gaol was the lesser punishment the butcher would receive that day.

A gaoler came by intermittently, but he was much more in

the mood to shout at Duncan rather than talk to him. Any explanation Duncan could offer fell on deaf ears.

Duncan hadn't broken into that study. He knew that. Major Hartley knew it. So why was he going to such lengths to get him arrested? How frightened must he be of Duncan's claim being successful if he thought that faking a crime and blaming him for it was the best option to stop it?

But that wasn't the worst thing.

He had no idea about Miss Hartley's condition. His stomach churned when he thought of her falling and hearing the panic-inducing crack as her head hit the stone. While she'd been conscious when he was taken away, he had no way of knowing what had happened since. Head wounds were particularly dangerous. That fight might well have been the last time he ever saw her.

He swore loudly and kicked at the closest thing, which happened to be a leg of the bed. The wood splintered quickly, its cheap manufacture giving no resistance to Duncan's force. The corner of the bed collapsed and the plate of food that had been resting on it crashed to the ground and alerted the guard when the metal clanged loudly.

"Oi, what're you doin'?" the man shouted, striding towards the cell. "That's malicious destruction of prifate property. Don't fink you're gettin' a new cell because you broke your bed."

"What are ye going tae do about it?" Duncan responded sardonically. "Arrest me?"

"Larf all you want, you're still stuck in 'ere. I ain't lettin' you out 'til they tell me to. Though I don't fink that'll be happenin', do you? You'll never be free again, like all the other good-for-nothin's who try to escape the law."

Duncan was ready to defend his honour and reiterate his innocence once again, but the gaoler was apparently happy with his remarks and walked away.

Duncan was left alone again in his tiny cell, now with a broken bed that he only had himself to blame for. He took a seat on the still intact half, trying to balance his weight so the rest didn't collapse as well.

As he sat, a familiar feeling began to rise in him.

It was infuriating to be stuck, helpless to actually do anything. He was cast back to his childhood years, unable to console his grieving mother when his father had died, unable to fight back against his uncle, unable to even save his beloved nanna from dying.

Unshed tears stung his eyes. There had been a darkness in him since he lost his nanna, and one that threatened to swallow him whole on a daily basis. He fought against it with all of his might, but the struggle was difficult. He found that growing closer to Miss Hartley had helped him considerably, bolstering him and proving there was still good in the world.

But now, alone, the darkness began to consume him. With no-one there to encourage him to defiance, make him see what was possible, his fears of insignificance, shame, and guilt rushed to the fore of his mind.

His chest grew tight as the dark demon shouted at him.

Yer useless.

Pathetic!

Naebody cares about ye.

Ye were never worth anything.

Yer a failure.

Yer uncle was right tae hate ye.

He pulled at his hair, curling into as tight a ball as he could on the hard, sloping cot. His breathing was fast and ragged.

Ye dunnae deserve tae be happy.

Ye'll never succeed.

Pitiful!

Ye only make life worse fer people ye meet.

Yer a poor excuse fer a man.

Miss Hartley wouldnae ever be able tae love ye.

Then, from the depths, came a song. Quiet and gentle at first, flowing like waves on a shore, washing away at the darkness. Soon the tune became stronger and he could make out the words.

Bee-o, Bee-o, bonnie, bonnie Bee-o
Bee-o, Bee-o, bonnie bairn o mine.

I love ma little laddie,
Yer just like yer daddy,
I love ye, I love ye,
I love ye 'cause yer mine.

The sound growing in power, he discerned his nanna's voice, a soothing timbre of thick Scottish that he felt in his soul. The music had a bittersweet tinge, a yearning for a lost loved one, but stronger was the comfort of a calming voice and memories of hugs and smiles.

The memories of his nanna renewed a strength in him. Despite his uncle's determined efforts to break him, there had always been a secret confidence that his nanna gave him — he just had to remember it was there.

He couldn't give in and let Major Hartley win. He had to fight back. There wasn't much he could do physically, but his rebellion started in his mind as he refused to let the Major's actions get to him and make him want to concede. He had to remind himself he hadn't done anything wrong, he didn't deserve this treatment, and there *were* people who supported him and believed him to be innocent.

That afternoon the gaoler came to speak to him.

"'You're lucky," he stated gruffly. "Someone wiff very deep pockets wants to talk to you." He turned away and spoke to a cloaked figure. "You've got a quarter of an 'our."

He grumbled back to his little office.

He'd hoped it was the magistrate coming to release him, but to his surprise it was actually Mrs Lutton. "I hope ye dunnae take it personally, ma'am, but yer the last person I expected tae see."

"No offence taken, my boy," replied Mrs Lutton. "I had only gone to Godshollow to discuss the ball with Miss Hartley — she was so worried about what you would think of our decorations. But when I arrived, I found a scene of pandemonium. Mr Peters was sweeping up broken glass in the courtyard, and Miss Hartley's maid was in a flood of tears about her mistress's injuries."

"How bad is Miss Hartley?" Duncan asked in distress. "Did ye see her?"

"I did. She is as well as can be expected. But I fear her future wellness is much in doubt."

Duncan wrung his hands together, pressing far harder than he should. "Dunnae say the doctor has pronounced it terminal," he begged. He hadn't been the one who pushed her, but he still felt responsible. Guilt would destroy him if the accident killed her.

Mrs Lutton looked confused for a moment. Then she snapped her fingers. "No, no," she assured him. "Her head is fine. Her brother believes she has lost her memory, but she is in fact totally well. No, the danger I worry for is that she has been engaged to that despicable Mr Ocheridge."

Duncan was angrier about the engagement than he would have been had she been dying. If the disdain in her voice when she had imparted that piece of information was anything to go by, Mrs Lutton felt much the same. A heavy stone dropped in his stomach and bile rose in his throat.

"She wouldnae agree to that," he protested.

"Quite right. They're taking advantage of this *memory loss* they think she has. I fear she has trapped herself."

Duncan took a deep breath. "What are ye expecting me tae be able tae do about this from in here? I havenae any proof I didnae break intae that study other than ma word."

"But Miss Hartley knows where you were. She told me everything. Why won't you tell the magistrate the truth? Miss Hartley would, but she fears it will disrupt her plans if she admitted it to her brother."

"I willnae have her ruin her reputation *fer ever* just tae get me out of gaol. The magistrate will find the truth."

"The magistrate is a busy man." she stated matter-of-factly. "And if the right price was suggested, the investigation could take a long time. If Miss Hartley gives her statement, you would get out of gaol today. She wouldn't need to keep up this engagement farce and you could both be happy."

Duncan couldn't control his anger. "Ye cannae be serious!" he snapped. "Do ye know what'll happen tae her? She willnae be able tae go out in public again. She willnae have a future. Even if we marry after I'm released, the stain of impropriety would be with her fer ever. I cannae believe ye agree with her."

Mrs Lutton smiled slyly. "You clearly care about her," she said with a glad undertone. "She cares about you too, so much that she's willing to do this to save you."

"Ye cannae justify it."

Mrs Lutton's lips pressed into a hard line. "That young woman trusts you. She is choosing you over her own family."

"That's exactly why I cannae let her do it," he cut in.

"You can and you will."

"Nae."

"So you're willing to doom both of you?"

"I would be if I followed yer plan."

"You're being unreasonable."

"Yer being short-sighted."

"There's no other option."

Duncan stopped. An idea hit him with the force of an out-of-control coal cart.

"Maybe there is," he suggested. Mrs Lutton didn't reply but lifted an eyebrow in expectation, so Duncan continued.

"Part of the charges is that I stole ma own papers from the study, aye?"

"Yes," Mrs Lutton affirmed.

"Obviously, I didnae steal the papers, so all ye have tae do is find them, and I'll be proved innocent."

Mrs Lutton's eyes lit up and she struck her forehead with her palm.

"How did I not think of that?" she mused aloud.

"Dunnae be too hard on yerself.

"That was a rhetorical question . . ."

Duncan liked her. She was a fiery woman. Much like his nanna, she knew her opinion and didn't apologise for it. She was tenacious and bold, and most importantly, she was willing to help him.

"Dunnae let Miss Hartley do anything before ye've looked fer the papers," he asked. "I cannae thank ye enough fer helping me. Maybe by the time I'm out of here, I'll have thought of a way tae repay ye."

"Don't you worry, young man," she replied with a smile. "I'm sure I can come up with some ideas as well."

He laughed. "I'm sure ye will." They drew silent and Mrs Lutton prepared to leave, Duncan stopped her just before she was gone.

"If she's feeling well enough, can ye bring her tae see me?"

Mrs Lutton promised she would try, and Duncan was left alone again.

CHAPTER SIXTEEN

Beatrice was in a very precarious position. While in the company of her brother and *fiancé* she was a blank slate. She'd been maintaining the illusion of memory loss and was letting them think their plot was succeeding.

That they thought they were getting away with their ridiculous plan was laughable. Jasper was excitable, like a child knowing they could have dessert after dinner, but Ocheridge was worse. He was strutting around like a peacock, smug and proud. Anyone would think he'd secured the rights to Godshollow, not a marriage.

She desperately wished to see Mr Mackenzie. Something had changed between them the night of the ball. Their conversation was so deep and personal there was no way they could've been the same afterwards. But she couldn't get out of the house. Jasper was using the excuse of her injury to keep her indoors, where she couldn't interfere with whatever they had planned, no doubt.

The only people who currently knew about her actual good health were the Luttons. Mrs Lutton had been to visit the morning after the ball to share gossip, and Beatrice had confided in her.

"He refused to let me tell the truth," she'd explained. "And like a coward I did as he asked. I should have spoken anyway. But now I can't say anything."

"A woman's reputation *is* all she has," Mrs Lutton replied.

"That's not why," Beatrice had replied. "I heard Jasper and

Ocheridge talking outside my room this morning before the doctor came. They've been planning something all along, and now, apparently, they're running out of time. It would seem once again that my brother has gotten himself into financial trouble and is running out of money too."

"What do you think they're up to?"

"I don't know. *That's* why I'm faking memory loss. They seemed desperate for me to have forgotten everything, so I figured that was my best plan to find out the truth. I can't tell the magistrate where Mr Mackenzie and I were when Miss Morton said he disappeared, or I jeopardise my attempts to foil Jasper in whatever he's doing."

Mrs Lutton had marvelled at her ingenuity. "But you are quite well?" she asked in concern. "What did the doctor say?"

"Apart from a large bump and a small headache, I'm perfectly fine. If Dr Allen knows about my trickery, he's keeping it quiet. He has thankfully told Jasper everything he wanted to hear."

"I applaud your skills as an actress."

"I just hope the magistrate is quick in his investigation. I wish I could talk to Mr Mackenzie. I want to help, but Jasper isn't going to let me anywhere near the gaol."

Mrs Lutton looked thoughtful. "I can go in your stead," she suggested. "I can talk to him. Perhaps I can convince *him* to tell of your balcony rendezvous if you cannot.

Beatrice had grasped her friend's hand tightly. "Would you?"

Beatrice had no idea when Mrs Lutton would be able to speak to Mr Mackenzie or when she would be back to report what had happened. She could do nothing but sit in the parlour and worry. She tried reading or sewing to occupy her mind, but to no avail.

Then, a little after five o'clock, she heard the sound of a

carriage in the courtyard. She was the first to the door to see who had arrived, Jasper no doubt too busy plotting with Ocheridge to be disturbed.

"Mr Daniels!" she cried happily when she opened the door for their guest. "It's so good to see you." She wrapped him in a hug. "Though I do wish it were under better circumstances."

Mr Daniels returned the hug but looked perplexed.

"I wouldn't say a new baby was dire circumstances," he replied. "All three of them are doing quite well over at Falton Bay, I would say. Though I see I've arrived in the middle of some sort of drama *here*. What on earth happened to the window?"

Beatrice tried to find the words to adequately explain the situation. "Well," she started trepidatiously. "When I returned from Mrs Lutton's ball, I learned the house was broken into. Jasper is trying to blame Mr Mackenzie, but I just know he didn't do that."

Mr Daniels was silent, no doubt mulling the information over in his mind.

"And who is Mr Mackenzie?" he asked.

Beatrice stopped in her tracks. "What do you mean?" she asked slowly. "Jasper said he put it all in his letter?"

"My dear, I haven't had any letters from your brother."

"No? He sent it weeks ago."

"It might be that it simply hasn't arrived yet," he postulated.

"No," Beatrice asserted. "He sent that letter before the baby was born. If you received a letter about the birth, you should have received his."

"Very strange," Mr Daniels commented. "It seems I'm a little behind on events here. Tell me everything."

"Well, perhaps we should get some tea and find Jasper. This is going to take some explaining. Oh, and he thinks that I don't remember anything about the break-in."

Jasper was less than forthcoming with information. He was emphatic that he'd sent Mr Daniels a letter about Mr Mackenzie, though something didn't feel right to Beatrice. He kept offering different ways the letter could have been lost, far too many, and this excess of excuses only served to make him look more and more guilty.

"I think we've established that a letter was sent," Mr Daniels said at length. "Perhaps now we can talk about what was *in* the letter?"

"Of course," Jasper said too enthusiastically. "Beatrice, would you leave us to talk please?"

"But—"

"*Now.*"

Mr Daniels tried to speak in her defence, but Jasper had an answer she couldn't argue against.

"Beatrice recently had a knock to the head which resulted in her losing her memory of the event. I don't what to risk her getting upset by talking her through it again. The doctor was very concerned that forcing the memories was to be avoided."

Mr Daniels looked at her with concern. She prayed he wouldn't realise that she'd accidentally proved that story to be false when she'd first greeted him.

"How considerate of you," he commended, much to Beatrice's relief "My dear, when we're finished, you and I can chat over some tea, and I'll tell you all about little baby Alfred."

So Beatrice left, though she'd been planning to stand outside the door to try and hear the nonsense Jasper was going to tell Mr Daniels. Unfortunately, her plans were interrupted by Mr Peters, who was coming to inform her of Mrs Lutton's arrival. He was surprised to learn of Mr Daniels's presence, but he was markedly cheerier when the knowledge had been imparted.

Mrs Lutton was waiting in the parlour, a very serious look on her face, when Beatrice entered.

"I've just come from the gaol," she stated.

Beatrice had fully intended to vent to Mrs Lutton about Jasper's behaviour, but the mention of the gaol wiped everything else from her mind.

"How is he?" she asked, hurriedly sitting down opposite her friend.

"About as well as can be expected under the circumstances."

Her heart ached. It was ridiculous that he was being punished like this. She was determined to do whatever she could to help him. "What did he think of our idea?"

Mrs Lutton raised an eyebrow. "What do Catholics think of Protestants?"

"I can't say I wasn't expecting that," Beatrice replied in exasperation. "But it's his best option. Where else is he going to find an alibi?" She'd risen from her seat and was pacing the floor, wearing out the rug before the fireplace.

"He did have one suggestion," Mrs Lutton offered. She explained Mr Mackenzie's thoughts about the papers.

As they discussed a plan to look for the papers, Beatrice felt anger rise within her again.

"I know that the potential loss of Godshollow is a big problem for Jasper right now, but I never thought he would stoop so low. I can't fathom a reason for him to take it this far. It would be inconvenient to have to find a new home, but not worth all this. Getting another man arrested isn't fair. I know Jasper's a sore loser, but I thought he still had *some* dignity left. He's in his study right now, no doubt spinning Mr Daniels a whole web of lies."

"Mr Daniels is here?"

"Yes, and I'm starting to think Jasper didn't send him a letter at all. He knows nothing about what's been going on here.

What could Jasper be up to? When did he become such a vindictive liar?"

"Perhaps it's not him controlling all of this," Mrs Lutton suggested.

"Ocheridge?" Beatrice mused. "Is he even smart enough to conceive this kind of plan? He's hardly the world's best lawyer. And what would he get out of it? I'm not being self-deprecating, but my hand in marriage certainly isn't worth this much underhandedness. What else does he stand to gain?"

"I think that at lot will be revealed if and when we find those papers," Mrs Lutton mused.

CHAPTER SEVENTEEN

The corridor to the burgled study was surprisingly empty. Even though she was the only one in the immediate vicinity, Beatrice was still quiet and swift. She didn't want anybody to know she was snooping. She'd left Mrs Lutton in the parlour, waiting to speak with Mr Daniels, whom she hadn't seen for a long while. From what Beatrice knew, the Luttons and Mr Daniels kept a regular written correspondence after a friendship had blossomed out of Annabelle's trauma, but only saw each other if there was time when Mr Daniels visited his niece.

When she arrived, she found the door unlocked. Looking inside, she found the study unchanged, as though the crime had only been committed the night before. Jasper had insisted that it be left as it was in case the magistrate wanted to look at anything again. The window still had the gaping hole of missing glass, the wooden slats that had been nailed over it providing only some resistance to the breeze which blew through the gaps, flapping the curtains and catching any loose sheets of paper, most of which had already been blown onto the floor.

She stepped through the doorway gingerly. The worst of the glass shards had been cleared up, but she was aware her house-shoes wouldn't offer the greatest protection if any had been missed.

She decided to start her investigation with the desk. That was the logical place to look for important papers. It may have seemed illogical to some to look in the place where the papers were reportedly stolen from, but she had to be sure that the papers really had been stolen. Jasper was behaving so strangely that she couldn't rule out that he was hiding the papers in that very room because he expected everyone to believe they were stolen — he was a soldier, he had to have learnt a thing or two about strategy and planning.

There wasn't anything obviously belonging to Mr Mackenzie at first glance, but she was prepared for a hunt. The large desk was supported by two columns of drawers, three apiece. A small hidden drawer concealed by an illusion front made the top seem thicker than it was.

Whoever had been in there the night of the *robbery* had pulled out all the drawers, but whilst the drawers had been haphazardly torn from the unit, the papers inside them looked neat and untouched, except for the top-right drawer. *That* had been searched, the contents disturbed. To Beatrice, this suggested the papers had been in that drawer and the burglar knew it — why else would none of the other papers be disturbed? They must have pulled the other drawers out to make the search seem more random but had forgotten about the papers in the drawers.

This placed Jasper fully in the line of suspicion. Only he knew where those papers were, so either he'd taken them himself, or he had told somebody else who then ransacked the office for show.

She felt sick. He had seemed so keen for Mr Mackenzie to stay when he first arrived — what had changed?

The dishevelled state of the drawer suggested the papers were already gone, but Beatrice wanted to search everything just in case. In truth, she wasn't entirely sure what she was looking for. What kind of paperwork would one bring with them to claim ownership of a house? If it was proof of lineage, it should have a family crest or something similar, but there was nothing fitting that description.

She couldn't find any paperwork with Mackenzie's name on it. There wasn't even any paperwork naming Godshollow.

She moved her search from the desk to the floor, kneeling carefully.

Then she found something.

Flapping from under a chair leg was a small paper folded in half, with *Hartley* written on the outside in brown ink, dated two weeks before Mr Mackenzie arrived. When she opened it, there were a list of names with amounts of money next to them.

Jefferies – £200
Carson – £350
Lettworth – £175
Butters – £250

At the bottom was a note:

Lord M has offered £1000, half of which will be yours upon completion of his request. All we have to do is keep him here until Lord M can arrive. This will cover most of the above debt and I will make a deal for the rest—Ocheridge.

This wasn't what she was looking for, but it appeared to be an important clue. Ocheridge and her brother had been given a task to complete. That would explain the comments about running out of time—perhaps this Lord M had given them a completion date. The £1000 reward was clearly Jasper's incentive.

Unfortunately, that note was all she found. There was nothing about Mr Mackenzie's lineage or about his family's ownership of Godshollow. Where else could she look?

A sound broke her from her internal reverie—footsteps. *Approaching* footsteps, too close for her to escape without being seen. She had precious few seconds to think of a good excuse for why she was there.

She jumped to her feet and tried to make herself seem as innocent as possible. She was just straightening the front of her dress when the door opened.

"Miss Hartley? What are you doing in here? You could get hurt."

Mr Ocheridge. Beatrice had to swallow her urge to run as far away from him as she could and faced him with a smile. An idea presented itself.

"There you are, Mr Ocheridge." She assumed her most coy attitude and offered him her hand, which he took and kissed. "Please don't tell my brother you found me here. I don't want him to worry."

"I could never betray a lady such as yourself. Though I am intrigued as to why you are so far from your usual environment. This is a man's domain. Not to mention it's in such a state since that awful Scotsman defiled it."

Good grief, the man was odious.

"That's the thing ... oh, it's so embarrassing." She wrenched her hands from his grip to cover her face in mock shame.

"Oh?" A thick smile curled his lips. "What an intriguing creature you are, Miss Hartley."

Beatrice didn't want to think about whatever scenario his limited imagination was conjuring up in that moment, but that meant her plan was working. Hopefully, she could flirt with him just enough to entertain his ego and make him forget she shouldn't be in there.

"All right," she said sweetly. "I'll tell you, but it must remain a secret. Just between us."

He grasped her hands. "Of course, my dear. I'm your fiancé, you can trust me."

She highly doubted that. Resisting an uncomfortable shiver that chased down her spine, she stepped closer to him, allowing him into her faux confidence.

"Well. Oh! It's so silly. You'll laugh at me. You see, I was looking for you. I couldn't find you anywhere, so I tried looking in here, as you and Jasper spend so much time here. Because of the bump on my head, I'd completely forgotten this room had been broken into. How silly is that?"

Mr Ocheridge's smile widened. He clasped her hands to his chest. "My dear, Miss Hartley, you needn't be embarrassed. You poor girl." He stood up straight and puffed his chest out. "We'll make sure that brutish Mackenzie receives just punishment for what he did to you."

Pushing down her repulsion, Beatrice started to lead him out of the study. "What a caring fiancé you are." She just about managed to say that without throwing up her breakfast, though it was *a near-run thing,* as the Duke of Wellington would say.

Mr Ocheridge perked up even more. If he were any happier, he'd have been skipping. Though he was making an obvious attempt to restrain himself, his protruding eyes bulged more than usual. Even under the copious amount of slicking agent, his hair appeared to move, thanks to the jiggling of his head caused by his excited trembling. "If I am, then it is because you make me," he postulated like a giddy schoolgirl.

The fight to stop herself from becoming sick was ever more difficult.

Spending any time with this repugnant man was last on the list of things Beatrice wanted to do. But perhaps she could charm some information out of him.

"Will you join me for some tea?"

Beatrice could only help but wonder how on earth Jasper had ever expected her to spend the rest of her life living with a man whose company she couldn't bear for even an hour. He was so monotonous and drudging—having a conversation with him was like swimming through very thick treacle with just about as little reward.

Before now, she would have thought it impossible for a person to be less exciting than unbuttered toast, but here she was.

He had tried to impress her by explaining various legal terms and situations. He loved talking, especially about himself. She'd hoped to use his overinflated ego to get information.

"It was a simple matter of legislative oversight," he pontificated in that dull, heavy voice. "Though it wasn't my error, you understand. My clerk was clearly at fault."

"Would that be Mr Tunstable?" she asked conversationally.

Mr Ocheridge's mood changed and his reply was short and sharp. "Why are you asking?"

That *wasn't* suspicious at all.

"From the stories I've heard, he sounds rather incompetent. Mr Mackenzie would have been much better off with *you* as his lawyer." He still looked suspicious. "If he wasn't a vicious villain, that is, and actually deserved any kindness."

The words felt wrong in her mouth. But she was now certain Mr Ocheridge had had a hand in whatever foul scheme Jasper was involved in. A fair assumption was, therefore, that if Mr Mackenzie's papers weren't in Jasper's office, the next logical place to look for them would be at the law firm. She just had to get there.

"You are such a wonderful lawyer," she lied. "I can't remember if I have already been, but I would love to see your office."

She had hoped that Mr Ocheridge would once again succumb to her charms, but he shook his head.

"I don't think that will be possible, dear. Even as my fiancée, you wouldn't be able to come alone. And your brother is a very busy man, far too busy to be chaperone for us."

"I'm sure Jasper wouldn't mind."

Mr Ocheridge continued to argue and eventually left the room. Beatrice had to find another way to get in.

Having been released from Mr Ocheridge's company, she went to find Mrs Lutton. She realised that she'd been gone far longer than they'd expected, and by now Mr Daniels should have finished with Jasper.

The two were deep in conference when she found them.

"Does she really? I think I need to meet this Mr Mackenzie."

Beatrice rushed forwards.

"I'll go with you."

Mrs Lutton gave Mr Daniels a look from the corner of her eye, then clapped her hands with glee. "What did you find, dear? Did you get the papers?"

Beatrice pulled the sheets out of her pocket. "No," she replied handing Mrs Lutton what she'd found. "But I know where to look next."

Mrs Lutton read the papers, with Mr Daniels watching over her shoulder. When they'd finished, they both fell silent.

Eventually, Mr Daniels spoke first. "What on earth has your brother been doing?"

"I can't say for certain," Beatrice admitted. "But I was thinking it over, and I might know who Lord M is. I would need to ask Mr Mackenzie to be sure."

"First thing in the morning, we will go to see him," Mr Daniels told her.

CHAPTER EIGHTEEN

Duncan had to wait until the next day to have any visitors. First was Major Hartley. His was a fleeting visit, purely done to parade the Major's feeling of superiority.

"I'm surprised ye waited so long tae come and gloat," Duncan stated when Hartley strode into the gaol.

"That's not the reason for my visit at all," was the reply.

"Then what *are* ye here fer?"

"I just wanted to extend you an invitation. In the unlikely event that you are released from prison, you are invited to attend the wedding of my sister to Mr Ocheridge."

Duncan clenched his fist and felt the heat rising to his head. "Ye cannae let her marry that bastard."

"There's nothing you can do about it. It's a prudent match, one that will solve a lot of problems."

"Aye, and none of them caused by her, I assume."

Major Hartley at least had the decency to look slightly guilty for a moment. "You don't know anything," he retorted. "And what happens to Beatrice is none of your concern. Indeed, in her eyes, *you* are the *bastard* here."

"What?"

Major Hartley grinned. "She has suffered from memory loss due to her bump on the head. She believes *you* were the one who pushed her."

Duncan remembered Mrs Lutton explaining the *memory loss*. Miss Hartley must be a brilliant actress. She had her brother believing every word. But Duncan had to be careful not to ruin the deception. He had to *believe* it as well.

"How bad is it?" he asked with as much desperation as he could muster. "Will the memories come back? What did the doctor say?"

"You have *no* right to care about her," the Major seethed.

"But I didnae push her, ye know that. I think I have every right tae care."

"Whether you had or not, you can't say that your reasons for being at Godshollow mean you care about any of us."

"I know ma claim doesnae exactly benefit ye, but I have nae personal quarrel with ye. I wasnae going tae rip yer home from ye just like that. I was at first ,but nae now. Yer sister has been incredibly kind tae me, and I wouldnae do anything tae hurt her."

Major Hartley waved a dismissive hand. "It's not something in your control anymore, so you don't have to worry about it. Have a good life."

He marched away.

Duncan's next visit came at nine o'clock and was much more pleasant.

He was greatly relieved to see Miss Hartley. She had come in with Mrs Lutton, but Duncan only had eyes for her.

"Are ye all right? Mrs Lutton said ye hadnae really lost yer memory, but how is yer head?"

Miss Hartley rushed forward and grasped his hands through the bars.

"I'm well," she assured him. "How are you? I do wish you'd let me tell them where we were. You shouldn't be in here."

Duncan looked between her and Mrs Lutton. "I couldnae ruin yer future. That kind of scandal would stick with ye always. Even if there was only a slight chance ye could get me out another way, I'd try a thousand low-odds schemes before I ruined yer name. Speaking of which, did ye find the papers?"

His heart sank when neither could give an affirmative answer.

"Not yet," Mrs Lutton said, confirming his fears. "But we're still looking."

"But what we *have* found is much more important," Miss Hartley added. "It was never highly likely that the papers would still be in that office, but I had to check. And I'm glad I did."

"What are ye talking about?"

"Well," Miss Hartley began. "Mr Daniels finally arrived."

"That's great," Duncan responded. "Is he here? What has yer brother told him?"

"Major Hartley, I'm afraid, didn't tell me anything."

An older man stepped forward. He wasn't what Duncan had pictured. He had a round, kind face and a largely bald head crowned by a ring of short grey hair, and he was rather more diminutive in stature — these recent events were really challenging his pre-conceived notions.

"Would it be inappropriate tae say it's a pleasure tae meet ye, Mr Daniels?"

"Probably, but I've never been an expert in that sort of thing." He extended his hand for Duncan to shake. "And neither, would it seem, is Major Hartley. I'm afraid I never received a letter from him, informing of your arrival and intentions or otherwise."

"I don't think he ever sent one at all," Miss Hartley cut in. "Have a look at these."

She turned to Mr Daniels, who reached into his bag and gave her papers, which she then handed to Duncan.

"This is a list of debts," he stated in confusion.

"It's the bottom bit that's important." She pointed to the note at the bottom. "This letter was dated not long before you arrived. Someone has offered them money to keep someone here — I'm presuming Godshollow or the area — until this Lord M can get here. I think they're talking about you."

Duncan couldn't believe it. "But who would want tae keep me here? And why?"

"You don't know who Lord M could be?" Miss Hartley asked hopefully.

"I dunnae know any lords," Duncan admitted. "If it is talking about me, the *m* may be fer Mackenzie. But there arenae any lairds in ma family. And with ma nanna gone, who in ma family would care where I was?"

Nobody had an answer. Though Duncan had a fear growing inside of him again. The same stories he'd been told as a child had been told to his uncle as well. This was the logical place for Duncan to go when he could stay in Scotland no longer. Did his uncle hope Duncan would make the claim and then he could ride down himself to seize the property from Duncan in the name of the family? Godshollow would certainly be a better income than the small pub the family owned.

But that was for Duncan to worry about. Right now, he needed Miss Hartley to look for his papers.

"I intend to visit Mr Ocheridge at work and see what I can find there. He's most probably at Godshollow with my brother, so I should get a chance to do a proper search. I may even get to meet Mr Tunstable."

Mrs Lutton coughed and stepped forwards. She gently put a hand on Miss Hartley's shoulder. "With that in mind, I think we should be heading there now. It was nice to see you again, Mr Mackenzie. We'll do everything we can to help you."

"Aye, and ye, Mrs Lutton. I'm sorry our first meeting wasnae under better circumstances, Mr Daniels."

Bows and curtseys were made, and Mrs Lutton ushered Mr Daniels away. At the last moment though, she turned and looked back. With a voice loud enough for the gaoler to hear, she spoke to Miss Hartley.

"Beatrice, dear, we'll meet you in the carriage. You tie your laces and catch up." Then she was gone, and Duncan was alone with Miss Hartley.

He knew they didn't have long, only the time it took to tie a shoelace, so he lifted her hands to his face and kissed them.

"Yer amazing, lass. I know this is hard fer ye, and I truly hope ye know that even if yer brother *is* involved, it doesnae change the way I feel about ye."

The hope in her eyes made his heart ache.

She reached forwards and gently kissed him on the cheek. "I will sort this all out, I promise."

Chapter Nineteen

As she made her way to the carriage, Beatrice tried to calm the warmness she could feel rising in her cheeks with swift wafts from her fan. She hid her face as she scuttled past the guard, who looked as though caring about anything would have been too much effort. She hated the thought of leaving Mr Mackenzie in that awful place, but if she was successful in her mission, he wouldn't be there much longer.

She was nervous getting into the carriage. Mr Daniels was one of the kindest souls she'd ever met, but even *he* couldn't be expected to like Mr Mackenzie under the circumstances.

She sat down next to Mrs Lutton, who gave her hand a reassuring pat.

"Mr Mackenzie seemed in good spirits," her friend commented. "Though I hope we find these papers. I don't like the thought of anyone staying in that place."

"We will. They *must* be in Ocheridge's office," Beatrice asserted. "When we get the papers, we'll be able to have Mr Mackenzie removed from that horrible gaol, and then we can put everything to rest."

Mr Daniels laughed and shook his head. "So this is what I'm missing when I'm away in Oxfordshire."

The gaol was on the other side of the town to the law office, so it took a while to get there. By the grand clock in the town square, it was five minutes before ten by the time they arrived.

When they knocked on the door, they were greeted by a woman.

"Yes?" she asked plainly.

Beatrice stepped forwards.

"We're here to see Mr Tunstable," she stated.

The woman frowned. "Not another one," she grumbled, turning to shout up the stairs. "Mr Widdersham, I need your help." She turned back to the three of them waiting on the doorstep. "You've got the wrong office. There's no Tunstable here. This is the office of Mr Widdersham and Mr Ocheridge, both of whom are in, if you would like to consult them on a legal matter."

Oh dear. Mr Ocheridge being in his office would make finding Mr Mackenzie's papers far more difficult. She didn't want her fiancé to be suspicious. Although that didn't mean she couldn't still look.

Mr Widdersham arrived quickly to offer assistance.

"What's wrong, Miriam?" he asked cautiously.

The woman tried to answer, but Beatrice wanted to speak before Tunstable could be mentioned again.

"I'm Miss Hartley," she supplied with a hand extended.

"I see." Widdersham's expression obviously said he didn't see at all, but he still shook her hand cordially. "And how can I help you?"

Beatrice hadn't expanded on her original introduction because she assumed Mr Ocheridge had told his business partner about the *engagement*, so an explanation wouldn't be needed. That was a perfectly reasonable assumption to make, though she considered that by this point, she really ought to know that Ocheridge didn't do things in a normal, or indeed reasonable, way.

Because the whole situation felt wrong, Beatrice didn't want to delve into a deep, long conversation that would raise a lot of awkward questions, but it seemed that Mrs Lutton didn't share her reserve.

"She's his fiancée, for goodness sake."

Surprise decorated Mr Widdersham's face, which changed to a smile

"Fiancée? That sly old thing. He didn't mention any courtship. I'd say he's done very well for himself. Let me take you up to his office."

Beatrice thanked him and he led the three of them upstairs. When he showed them into Ocheridge's office, he seemed confused.

"Miss Hartley, it's wonderful to see you. You look positively effervescent," he gushed loudly. Then he lowered his voice slightly. "It's such a nice surprise, but I thought we'd agreed you wouldn't visit me at work?"

Beatrice played dumb. "Did we? I'm sorry, my memory is all over the place. The doctor did say I might struggle with immediate memories."

"But we had that conversation only recently."

This just confirmed to Beatrice that she was right in thinking the papers would be here. He was acting as though he had something to hide, as well he might.

"Well, Mr Daniels wanted to come and see you, and I just got so excited it must have completely slipped my mind."

"Now really isn't a good time, *dear.*"

"Come now, Ocheridge," Mr Widdersham cut in. "You're a lucky man to have a fiancée interested in your work! My Doris can't bear it if I try to talk to her about my cases. She likes the gossip, mind you, but she's not so eager to know the ins and outs of life as a lawyer. What could be the harm in letting her see where you work?"

"When you put it that way," Ocheridge replied through gritted teeth, "I'm very lucky. Come in, but this will have to be quick." He swiftly swept Beatrice and her companions into his office, firmly shutting the door.

He stood in the middle of the room, daring her to try and make it past him to his desk. "Here you are, darling. Though

I'm afraid it isn't much to look at. Why don't you wait outside now whilst I talk to Mr Daniels?"

"Oh, but it's so lovely," Beatrice insisted, brazenly pushing her way further into the room. "You two talk, and we'll just look around." She beckoned Mrs Lutton over to the wooden desk. "Our father had a bureau so much like this. I remember when I was little, I thought it was magic. So many little drawers and cupboards."

Beside her, Mrs Lutton had spotted a pile of papers and began to leaf through them. "This is an awful lot of cases," she remarked. "You must be very busy."

"I am," Ocheridge replied hastily. "And I'd rather you didn't touch them." As he snatched the papers from Mrs Lutton's hands, Beatrice saw a corner of one sheet which was decorated with a family crest. Ocheridge placed the pile on a nearby chair.

"Of course, my love," she replied with sickening placation. "We won't touch anything. You won't even know we're here. Let's take a look out the window, Mrs Lutton. It must be a lovely view from here." She crossed the room and stood in front of glass that was smudged and dusty, pretending to enjoy the view as the gentlemen started to talk.

The view was, in fact, very dull, facing the back of what looked to be a public park a yard away. The view would have been nice, but the plants were overgrown and untended. What once had been green was becoming brown, and the railings were covered with large spots of coppery rust. In short, it was a view that wouldn't have inspired even the most brilliant of poets.

She watched the view intently, trying to think of a way she could get her hands on those papers. A few children were playing in the park, running with their kites held aloft by a stiff breeze.

When Mrs Lutton reached her side, she dropped her voice

to a whisper.

"We're never going to get to look around for those papers while *he's* in here."

"Indeed," her friend replied in similarly hushed tones. "But how can we find a way to be in here without him?"

Beatrice turned back to the view as she pondered the question. The kite of one young boy became stuck in a tree, its string having become snagged on a branch. As he and his fellows pulled, the movement began to loosen the knots and unravel.

That presented Beatrice with the idea for a plan. She slowly moved away from the window, and as subtly as she could, she pulled on the ribbon that kept her dress fastened. As soon as the fastenings began to loosen, she cried out.

"Oh . . . oh my! Mrs Lutton, I need your help."

"Are you all right?" Her concerned friend rushed to her side.

Beatrice clutched the front of her bodice. "No," she replied dramatically. "My dress has come undone. The ribbon must have caught on the window latch."

"Oh goodness," Mr Daniels exclaimed. "Can I help?"

Mrs Lutton had caught on to Beatrice's plan and tutted scoldingly.

"No, no, this is a woman's job. And with that in mind, I'll need to ask you gentlemen to leave."

"Leave?" Ocheridge objected. "This is *my* office!"

"That's as may be," Mrs Lutton countered. "But I'll have to undo the whole thing and start again, which may reveal Miss Hartley's underthings. Do you really want word getting out that you were in your office with a half-dressed young woman?"

Ocheridge began to splutter with embarrassment. He led Mr Daniels out of his office in a heartbeat.

"Well done, Mrs Lutton," Beatrice commended as she ran

to the pile of papers. "That was outstanding."

"I could have done better if I'd been briefed on the plan," Mrs Lutton said pointedly.

"I'm sorry, it just came to me. I didn't have time to explain. And we don't have much time now. Please start searching." Beatrice raced her fingers through the pile she'd noticed before as she frantically searched for the crest again.

"Oh dear, silly me," Mrs Lutton said loudly as she investigated the desk. "I've laced it the wrong way. I'll have to start all over again or you'll be terribly uncomfortable."

For all of her outward appearances as an elderly gentlewoman, Mrs Lutton was a wonderful accomplice.

A knock sounded on the door.

"How long is this going to take?" was Ocheridge's question.

"Nearly finished," Mrs Lutton called back. "It's a tricky process, you know."

They hadn't much time left. Beatrice pulled the rest of the papers out of the pile and handed them to Mrs Lutton.

"Quickly," she said. "Put these in the back of my dress."

"What?" It took a moment for Mrs Lutton to follow Beatrice's instructions. "Oh, yes, yes."

More impatient knocking at the door.

Beatrice's heart was racing. She held her breath as Mrs Lutton did as she was bade, only just managing to do up the dress before Ocheridge decided he wasn't going to wait any longer.

"All done," Mrs Lutton announced as the door opened. "Is that comfortable for you, dear?"

"Very much," Beatrice answered. She gave a very unimpressed-looking Ocheridge an apologetic smile. "I'm so sorry. I can see we've made a nuisance of ourselves. We should go, Mrs Lutton, leave the men to their business. I saw an inn along the way. We can wait there for you, Mr Daniels."

She quickly took Mrs Lutton's hand and led her out.

"Sorry again," was her farewell.

Beatrice only felt safe when she and Mrs Lutton were around the corner and out of sight of the office. Then she stopped and let out a deep breath.

"That was terrifying," she admitted. "My hands are shaking."

"As were mine," Mrs Lutton replied. "Makes it terribly hard to tie ribbon."

"Do you think he suspected anything?"

"I don't know, my dear. He *is* a bit dim. But I fear we were hardly exactly subtle."

"Let's just hope the papers we took were the right ones. We won't be able to try again."

They made their way to the inn. After retrieving the papers in privacy, they sat at a table with a drink—the innkeeper wouldn't let them sit without one—and looked through them.

"Marvellous." Mrs Lutton leafed through her half of the pile. "These are ancestry documents. We've got family trees and crests." She laid out a piece of paper on the desk. "There's our Mr Mackenzie, I should think." She pointed to a name at the bottom. Under Marcus and Judith was a single line leading to Duncan.

Beatrice laughed happily. She traced the little black line farther up the page. "Fraser Mackenzie. 1599-1649. This is the man who built Godshollow?"

"Yes," Mrs Lutton agreed. "If this is anything to go by." She put another piece of paper in front of Beatrice.

"It's the original deed!" she exclaimed. "Ocheridge had it all along. How stupid of me. When I was looking at the records at Godshollow, it didn't occur to me that the lack of dust on the books meant they'd been read recently. Why did he have them, though?"

She went back to her pile of papers to see if there was

anything else useful. The last page stopped her breath.

A. Ocheridge Esq.
I am sorry to hear that Mr Tunstable has been so long retired. However, I think this change may prove advantageous.

I suspect that my nephew, Duncan Mackenzie will be coming to Godshollow. He may well seek you out, as Mr Tunstable was the man who informed our family of the property. I cannot say when he will arrive. I expect it will be in the near future. Know that when he arrives, I shall only be about three weeks behind.

My nephew will be making this trip in the hopes of claiming it as an heir of Fraser Mackenzie, who built the property.

This must not be allowed to happen. As head of the family, that is my right. He is the son of second son, jealous and bitter, seeking — as his father did — to take what is rightfully mine. However, my interfering old mother has seen fit to hide from me that which would authenticate a claim. I suspect my nephew has it. I ask you that you obtain this evidence from him and detain him from making his claim by whatever means necessary until I arrive to make the claim myself.

For this task I will offer the reward of £3000.

I recommend you continue to let him believe Mr Tunstable is still handling the case. Keep your involvement undisclosed.

As proof of my legitimacy, you will find the original deed to Godshollow in a secret room hidden behind a bookshelf on the top floor of the West Wing where my ancestors hid it.

Laird Graeme Mackenzie.

CHAPTER TWENTY

Honestly, Duncan hadn't expected to see Miss Hartley again that day. Not that he didn't trust her, or didn't believe her capable, but he was a pessimist by nature.

Once she left, he'd been alone with his thoughts, and they all were focussed on Graeme Mackenzie. Could he really believe his uncle hated him *that* much, and wanted Godshollow enough that he would write to complete strangers and persuade them to have him arrested?

But he hadn't told his uncle he was even leaving, let alone where he was going. How would he know to send word ahead?

The argument circled viciously in his mind, racing backwards and forwards, enough to make him dizzy.

He just needed to get out of the gaol. If he wasn't confined like this, he wouldn't be trapped inside his own mind. In here, he had nothing else to do but to think, and his thoughts were his own worst enemy.

He lay down on his half-collapsed cot and closed his eyes. He tried to picture himself somewhere else, anywhere else. He forced himself to think of blue skies, green fields, and a warm breeze. But his efforts were for naught when a loud commotion disrupted his concentration.

He could hear the gaoler arguing with a group.

"You've already seen 'im once today. You ain't gittin' to see 'im again."

That caught his attention.

"What twaddle, sir," replied a man's voice. "We have

every right to see him again. You are standing in the way of justice."

"I ain't doin' nuffink. You can't visit twice. You'll 'ave to come back in the mornin'."

"Nonsense."

"I've got the key. I'm in charge. I make the rules."

Two female voices added their disapproval to their companion's. Duncan was certain this was Miss Hartley and her two helpers, and he could honestly say he'd never felt better in his life.

"I wannae see them," he shouted, letting them all know he could hear them.

"You don't git a say," the gaoler shouted back.

"But, sir, we have the proof of his innocence. He shouldn't be locked up any longer."

That was definitely Miss Hartley's voice. They'd found the papers!

"You can't do nuffink wiff-out the magistrate," the gaoler protested. "Get 'im 'ere tomorrow mornin' and I might be able to git 'is case reviewed. Though it'll 'ave to be very convincin' evidence."

"Oh, we will," Mrs Lutton promised loudly and menacingly. "Fear not, Mr Mackenzie. We will return at first light tomorrow."

"I'll be waiting fer ye," Duncan shouted back. He loathed having to spend another night in this miserable place, but that was his only choice.

"We found what you wanted," Miss Hartley added. "They'll *have* to release you. Stay strong until then."

"I will, lass."

That night had been the most difficult of Duncan's life. Everything seemed so close now, and yet felt as far away as ever. He was full of nervous tension that wouldn't let him rest. If he tried to sleep, nothing would calm him, and he couldn't let his mind drift into unconsciousness.

When morning came, his anxiety increased. The hours he waited felt like days, but eventually Miss Hartley arrived, magistrate in tow. Duncan was released from the cell by a very begrudging gaoler, but instead of being shown out of the prison, he was given a seat with the magistrate.

"You know why you were taken into custody, Mr Mackenzie?"

"Aye, ye were there."

The magistrate raised an eyebrow. "I would like to hear it in your own words."

Duncan complied. "I was accused of breaking intae a study tae steal some papers."

"And you refute these accusations?"

"I do."

"What is your defence?"

"I was at a ball at the time they say the burglary was committed. I also dunnae have the papers I was accused of stealing."

"Yet you refuse to name a witness who can corroborate your story."

"I was taking a breath of air. There was nae other person with me."

"I see. And what about the papers?"

"They were ancestry papers. Ma friends should have shown them tae ye."

"They have. Do you know a Mr Ocheridge?"

"I do. He's a lawyer here in town and a friend of Major Hartley."

"And Mr Tunstable?"

"Another lawyer. He has been helping with ma case."

"I see. Finally, you tell me about your uncle?"

Duncan's heart stopped.

"What about him?"

"What kind of a man was he? What was your relationship like?"

"Why are ye asking about him though?"

"Just answer the question."

"I dunnae want tae talk about him. He hated me."

The magistrate paused again. "You say hated, past tense. Is he no longer with us?"

"He's still alive, but I fully intend on never having tae see him again."

"Very well." He rose from his seat, gesturing for Duncan to do the same. "Mr Mackenzie, from the evidence presented to me and your testimony, I have reason to doubt the validity of the claims made against you. I will investigate the matter myself. And until such time as I reach a decision, you are released from this gaol, but you may not leave the area. Is that understood?"

"Aye, sir," Duncan asserted with relief. "That's wonderful. Thank ye so much fer believing me."

"It's not a question of my believing you. You need to thank your friends, Mr Mackenzie. Their evidence was very hard to disbelieve."

He walked Duncan out to where Miss Hartley, Mrs Lutton, and Mr Daniels were waiting.

"Mr Colin Daniels, I, Magistrate Malcolm Klaxley, do hereby release Mr Duncan Mackenzie into your custody until such time as a decision can be reached regarding this case. He is not to leave this county. If he does, there will be severe repercussions for both of you. Do you accept this?"

"I do."

"Then I bid you good day. I *will* be seeing you again." He walked away to his carriage, leaving Duncan alone to thank his saviours.

He was so overwhelmed with emotion he couldn't stop

himself from scooping Miss Hartley into a big hug, almost pulling her off the ground.

"Is that how we're all to be thanked?" Mrs Lutton asked jokingly. "I don't think my brittle old bones could take that."

"Ye know yer the strongest of all of us, Mrs Lutton." Duncan released Miss Hartley to shake the other woman's hand and then Mr Daniels's. "How can I thank ye fer helping Miss Hartley get me out of there?"

"I think first we need to get you to Godshollow and get you fed. Let's just get you home."

She led him to the waiting carriage, and Duncan felt like he could finally relax.

CHAPTER TWENTY-ONE

Beatrice was full of mixed emotions. She was happy, over-joyed they'd been able to prove Mr Mackenzie's innocence and free him, but she felt dread, apprehension, and even anger about Jasper's role in what had occurred over the past months.

When she'd returned to Godshollow with Mr Daniels after they'd ferried Mrs Lutton to Havenbrooke the night before, Beatrice hadn't told Jasper anything about what they'd done that day, other than the visit to Mr Ocheridge's office. He had, in fact, already been informed of the incident by Mr Ocheridge himself, who had invited himself to dinner.

He hadn't been best pleased with her choice of activity, and even tried to chastise Mr Daniels for taking her adventuring when she was in such weak health. She had nearly dropped her ruse then, so angry was she. But Mr Daniels's calm presence beside her helped to keep her from destroying all of her hard work.

She even managed to stay silent when Mr Ocheridge joined the conversation. She was going to be very glad when she didn't have to play fiancée to that ill-mannered, conniving, slimy weasel.

"I do hope you aren't too tired after your excursion today, Miss Hartley," he'd said with sickeningly false attention. "Perhaps it would be best for you to stay at home for the next few days to rest."

That had struck her as odd, being such a specific

suggestion, but she'd kept her apprehensions to herself for the moment.

"You don't have any more plans to go out, do you?" Jasper had asked patronisingly.

At times, since the accident, Beatrice had wondered if some of Jasper's affection towards her and his concern was genuine. But now that she realized what he and Ocheridge were doing, she couldn't interpret their behaviour as anything other than malicious.

"I'll be careful," she had placated him. She tried to keep her voice as level and emotionless as possible.

"You'll do better than that," Jasper rebutted. "I'm going to keep my eye on you tomorrow. I'll make sure you won't leave the house."

"But—"

"Until the doctor clears you, I am *not* going to let you put your health at risk."

She could have argued for much longer on the issue, but she honestly didn't have the energy.

She knew Jasper was going to be furious when he discovered she'd snuck out again. He was also going to be mad when it came to light that she'd stolen papers from Mr Ocheridge. He was going to be *livid* when she revealed she didn't have any memory loss. And he'd be apoplectic when she returned home with Mr Mackenzie following.

But as angry as he would get with her, he would never rival the fury she had towards him. To think he'd conspired to do what had been done and put another person's freedom, possibly their life, at risk was beyond anything she could tolerate. His anger would seem like mild annoyance by comparison to her own.

As they drew closer to Godshollow, her confidence grew. Jasper couldn't fight the evidence they had, and his scheming would be revealed as such. She was ready to charge in, to confront Jasper and have the whole thing out before dinner time, but Mr Daniels held her back.

"We need to do this carefully," he advised her quietly as they exited the carriage. "We need to tell Mr Mackenzie what we know and follow his lead."

She agreed that was the fairest thing to do. She dreaded telling Mr Mackenzie about his uncle — he'd suffered so much already. Nevertheless, he needed to hear it, and it would probably be best if she was to tell him.

Mrs Lutton went in first, on the lookout for Jasper, prepared to jump in and distract him if needed. Next went Beatrice, followed by Mr Mackenzie, and the group was rounded out by Mr Daniels.

"It's like being on manoeuvres again," the former brigadier commented jokingly.

They moved in short bursts of travel, risking one hallway at a time, always checking to see if the coast was clear before moving on. Eventually, they arrived at Mr Mackenzie's room, but now they found themselves with a problem — the door was locked. No doubt Jasper had had the room sealed as soon as Mr Mackenzie had been taken away, preventing prying eyes.

This forced them to readjust their plan. Instead, they decided to take him to Beatrice's room. All things considered, that was probably the best option anyway. Having a bath drawn in *her* room would not be unexpected. Both she and Jasper had bathing rooms attached to their bedrooms, so that was where they bathed. Picking a random empty bathing room would seem suspicious. Poor Mr Mackenzie had suffered enough and deserved to feel clean.

The room required twenty minutes to be readied for bathing, especially when trying to keep the servants out of the bedroom. They relented eventually, thanks to Beatrice's fondness for pouring herself a bath in the past—she found the process soothing. Beatrice entered with the hot water to find Mr Mackenzie lying on her bed dozing. She had half a mind to let him continue to rest. But really, they needed to get so much done that this was a luxury they couldn't indulge in.

She gently placed a hand on his shoulder and shook him awake. Bleary-eyed, he rolled off of the bed and followed her into the bathing room attached to the bedroom.

"I'll just be through in the other room with Mr Daniels if you need any . . . help." That was then that she realised just what was going to be happening. A very handsome man was going to be naked while she was only a few feet away in the conjoining room, a small door being the only thing to protect his modesty.

She tried not to think about that, but the idea always wormed its way back into her mind. Thank goodness Mr Daniels was with her to talk to.

"Thank you for all your help," she told him. "I'm sorry to have put you in such a difficult position."

Mr Daniels smiled and nodded. "You're welcome, my dear. Don't be sorry. True, it is a very odd situation. But ever since I came into possession of this place, it's been one bizarre event after another." He patted her shoulder affectionately then took her by the elbow. "Why don't you go and find some clothes for Mr Mackenzie, and give him some privacy? I'll stand guard in the hall lest anyone comes snooping."

He was right. Mr Mackenzie probably wouldn't want to wear the same dirty garments he'd worn in the gaol. But with the door to his room locked, how was she going to get him fresh clothes?

She pondered the issue before deciding she would simply have to *borrow* some for him, Jasper would be the best option. Her first choice was to ask Mr Daniels, but he rightfully pointed out that he was a good foot shorter than Mr

Mackenzie and nowhere near as muscularly developed. There was no time to send Mrs Lutton for some of the General's clothes, so Jasper remained the only option.

She dashed to Jasper's room, praying that her brother was occupied elsewhere. Fortune was smiling on her — she found his room empty.

After a few moments, she managed to collect a good assortment of clothing, including breeches, a shirt, a cravat, socks, and a waistcoat. Jasper valued uniqueness in his coats, so she decided she'd better not purloin one of those as well, or Jasper would twig straight away from where she had sourced the outfit.

When she re-joined Mr Daniels, he smiled at her bundle.

"Just in time," he told her. "Mr Mackenzie said he was ready to finish."

Beatrice laid the pile of clothes on the floor before the door, informing Mr Mackenzie as she did what she had found for him to wear. "We'll be waiting in the hall. Join us when you're ready."

There was the sound of water splashing and settling as it did when someone emerged from it. He came out of Beatrice's room to join them a few minutes later looking a lot cleaner and more comfortable.

Washed and dressed, Mr Mackenzie was ready to be told what had been uncovered. Mr Daniels let Beatrice take the lead.

"I'll go and see if I can find Mr Mackenzie some food," he offered, leaving the two of them in the doorway.

First Beatrice handed Mr Mackenzie the ancestry papers, which he received with great relief. Then it was time to talk about the letter. She fingered the sleeve of her dress as she thought best about how to phrase what she needed to tell him. She had spent hours the night before thinking up all the different ways she could impart the news, but now her mind couldn't bring any of her scripts to mind.

She reached out and grasped his hand comfortingly. "We found something else along with the papers," she started hesitantly. "A letter. To Mr Ocheridge. From your uncle."

"I suspected as much. I just hoped fer once that I could be in charge of ma own future. I guess I'll nae ever be free of him."

"No," Beatrice proposed vehemently. "You *are* free of him. Even though he has tried to orchestrate things, he's failed. We've gotten you free from gaol, and we'll get you Godshollow. By the time he arrives, there will be nothing he can do. You're not a child anymore over whom he has ultimate power. He can't do anything to you now. Don't you dare let him beat you."

He smiled at her weakly. "Ye cannae be certain of that. Ma uncle is a force ye've nae ever dealt with before. He doesnae care what he has tae do tae get his way."

"Then we will counter anything he throws at us."

"Us?" he repeated uncertainly. "I do appreciate everything ye've done fer me, lass, but I cannae ask ye tae do any more."

Beatrice laughed. "You don't have to ask," she replied warmly. "I'm going to do it anyway."

"But ye dunnae understand. Ma uncle is *dangerous*."

"So am I, when the need arises."

"This isnae a game." He sounded desperate and scared.

She held his face between her hands and looked him dead in the eye. "I am *not* letting you do this alone. There's nothing you can do to stop me, and nothing that doesn't make me involved. My brother is connected to all of this, too. And if it makes you feel better, I'm fighting on those grounds."

He couldn't argue with her.

She saw the acceptance in his countenance and knew she had won her case, though her resolve was quickly put to the test when Mrs Lutton came to join them and Mr Daniels returned without food.

"Beatrice dear, I was intercepted on my mission by your brother. He would like to speak with you. We can't hide Mr Mackenzie any longer. Are you ready?"

"Oh, there's a lot I'd like tae say tae him," Mr Mackenzie replied.

"I know," Beatrice said tentatively. "I want to shout and curse at him too, but I don't think there is anything to be gained by fighting with him right now."

"Quite so," Mr Daniels seconded. "You have every right to an audience with the Major, Lord knows you do, but this is a very delicate situation. The calmer we are, the less Major Hartley has to use against us. We don't want you giving him any reasons to have you sent back to gaol."

"Yer right," Mr Mackenzie conceded, much to Beatrice's relief. "I cannae make too many promises, but I will try and remain in control of ma emotions."

The group made their way to the drawing room, where Jasper first greeted them with a smug grin that quickly changed to shock when Mr Mackenzie made his entrance.

"What's going on?" he snapped, visibly panicked.

"Mr Mackenzie has been released from the gaol," Beatrice stated matter-of-factly, trying to keep her voice level.

"How? Why? What did you do, you stupid girl?"

"Hey," Mr Mackenzie exclaimed back. "Dunnae talk tae her like that."

"Don't *you* tell *me* what to do," was the childish comeback.

"Could we stop with all the shouting please?" Beatrice asked. "Sit down, Jasper, let's talk about this civilly."

"No," he defied. "That man's dangerous. He pushed you."

"That wasnae me, ye scunner!"

"What did you call me?"

"Ye heard me."

"That's enough!" Mr Daniels commanded, bringing the men to silence. "It has been proven that Mr Mackenzie is innocent of the crimes he was charged with. He is here as my guest, and I expect you to conduct your business with him with as much decorum as you would with anyone else."

"You can't expect me to —"

"Yes, I *can*. And you *will* do as I ask."

Beatrice was mightily impressed with Mr Daniels. She had never seen anyone other than their father deal with Jasper so successfully.

"Now, let's sit down and discuss this like gentlemen . . . and lady," Mr Daniels said calmly.

Beatrice could tell Jasper wanted to argue that he didn't want her to be there, but a look from Mr Daniels stopped the words in his throat. He really was an impressive leader.

With everyone seated around the table, Mr Daniels began the discussion.

"We all know what it is we're here to talk about. I am fully aware of Mr Mackenzie's intentions, as I have heard from yourself, Major Hartley. This is a very serious matter, and I want to hear every side of the story before I can come to a judgement. It would certainly be easier to decide this between ourselves than to take it through the courts."

"You can't be seriously considering his claim?" Jasper baulked.

"It cannot be discounted. The paperwork is very compelling."

Jasper pulled a face that nearly had Beatrice in tears of laughter. "Paperwork? You've seen paperwork?"

"You sound surprised," Mr Daniels commented. "You didn't think Mr Mackenzie would turn up to make such a claim without the proper evidence."

Jasper was at a crossroads. Beatrice could see him weighing the options. He would have to either accept Mr Daniels's assertion or admit that Ocheridge had the papers all along.

"Of course not," Jasper said at length. "They *were* in my office for safekeeping, but after the break-in, they disappeared. As it has been *proved* that it wasn't Mackenzie who committed the crime, I was doubtful that we would ever see the papers again."

That was a quick lie which none believed, but for the sake of peace, the lie was left alone.

"Fortunately," Mr Mackenzie replied sharply, "that wasnae the case."

Jasper didn't respond.

"What did you make of the papers, Mr Daniels?" Beatrice asked, trying to get the conversation back to topic and leave behind the next argument brewing between the two young men.

"They are certainly credible," he answered truthfully. "I suppose the issue is whether we should honour the original owner or the Lord Protector's ruling. As the ruling was made by a leader whose laws were later repealed by the returning monarchy, I'm inclined to favour the original deeds. However," —he continued before anyone else could interrupt— "those laws were legally repealed with documentation for most places seized by Cromwell, and there's no evidence of that happening in this case.

"It's not a simple issue. I suppose what it really comes down to is that as I am the current owner of this property, I am the one who is in charge here."

"Exactly," Jasper agreed hurriedly. "That means that you have no responsibility to even listen to this *supposed legatee*."

"But that means he has every right to, as well," Beatrice countered.

"Why are you defending this man, Beatrice? You realise what this would mean for us."

"Of course I do," she replied defensively. "But it's not

about what *we* want. We're only tenants. Mr Daniels doesn't have to seek our approval to do anything with the property."

"But I would certainly never do something so drastic without at least consulting you first," Mr Daniels pointed out. "That is the reason for this meeting, surely?"

"It is," Jasper responded. "I had just assumed that you would see sense and take our side."

"*Our* side?" Beatrice questioned testily. "You don't speak for me."

"What is this betrayal? How can you even think of supporting this madman?" Jasper demanded.

"Because, unlike Mr Mackenzie, we have other options. *I* can stay with Charles and Annabelle, *you* can return to the army, and *Mr Daniels* has his home in Oxfordshire. Mr Mackenzie has nothing."

Jasper laughed derisively. "What manner of sentimental lies has he been spinning you? Has your bump on the head made you gullible as well as forgetful?"

"Jasper, I didn't forget anything. I heard you talking to Ocheridge about how fortuitous it would be if I *had* forgotten. I wanted to know what you were doing, so I made you believe so. Though part of me wishes I'd never learnt anything about your sordid little scheme. I'm disappointed in you, Jasper. And our father would have been too."

That was a horrible thing to say to him, but her brother had done horrible things. The words had their desired effect, and Jasper stopped protesting. He looked defeated.

"I didn't have another choice," he said finally. He wasn't cross. There was no shouting. He spoke with the confidence of a man who thought he'd been doing the right thing. "We need the money—you can't run a place like this without spending. At first, businessmen in town were happy to give me an account, but now they're asking for the money back, and we don't have it. When Ocheridge wrote to me about

Lord Mackenzie, I thought I'd found the answer. He was offering enough money to pay off all our debts. This seemed like an easy job."

"*Our* debtors?" Beatrice seethed. "I found your list, Jasper. I've never had dealings with those people or those businesses. I don't even know who they are."

"It's none of your business who they are," Jasper retorted.

"And yet it's *our* debt. Who are they? Were these debts derived from gambling? From buying alcohol? Because I had nothing to do with any of that. That's *your* debt, not *ours*."

"You want to see me go to debtor's jail?"

Beatrice was seething. She was ready to give Jasper the telling-off of his life, but Mr Daniels cut in with his calm demeanour.

"Then why the nonsense with the break-in?" the older man asked plainly.

"I was running out of time. Two weeks after Mr Mackenzie arrived would be the day after tomorrow. Plus, Charles's baby had been born. That meant Mr Daniels would be on his way as well. I never wrote when Mr Mackenzie arrived. I was going to wait for his uncle, so Mr Daniels knew nothing of the first Mackenzie. Mackenzie's papers proved what his uncle had told us was a lie, he wasn't the son of a second son, he was the heir. But we needed the money. I had to do something."

"False imprisonment?" Mr Mackenzie asked incredulously. "I could have hanged fer theft."

"I wouldn't have let it go that far," her brother had the gall to defend. "Lord Mackenzie will be arriving any day now. Once he arrived, I would have gotten *Mr* Mackenzie released."

"That isnae good enough," Mr Mackenzie fumed. "Do ye know he isnae even a laird? He owns an inn in Cromarty. He cannae pay ye £3000, he probably doesnae even have £300."

Jasper spluttered in shock and tried to argue.

"You're lying," he accused Mr Mackenzie.

"Nae. I promise ye. Our family may have been influential in court, but we havnae had high status fer a long time. When Laird Fraser was killed, the Mackenzies had nothing. We've been innkeepers ever since."

"Then it was all for nothing," Jasper responded slowly. "I put in all that work and was never going to get the money."

Something in Beatrice snapped. Her brother seemed much more upset about the lack of monetary reward than what he'd actually done.

"How dare you," she seethed. "Mr Mackenzie could have hanged for a crime like theft. You could have killed him, Jasper. And all you seem to be upset about is that you might not get paid for it?"

She moved around to stand right in front of him. She didn't allow him to respond.

"You're disgusting." The anger overtook her and she slapped Jasper as hard as she could, so hard that her hand stung. "I don't want anything more to do with you. I refuse to be your sister."

She left the room, tears running down her cheeks. She marched through the halls, not stopping until she came to her bedroom. She sat down at her vanity and stared at herself in the mirror.

How could she be related to someone who could be that underhanded and cruel? She saw the same green eyes that she, Jasper, and their father had shared. The same dark hair covered her head and his. Her reflection was taunting her.

She wasn't sure how long she'd been sitting in front of the mirror when somebody knocked on her door.

"Who is it?" she asked.

"Mr Mackenzie."

"Come in." She watched him enter through the mirror, never turning.

He walked up to her and placed his hand on her shoulder. "How are ye, lass?" he probed gently.

Beatrice sighed. "I'm angry," she replied.

"I know. Yer brother isnae faring too well either," Mr Mackenzie replied.

"I don't care," she answered bluntly.

Mr Mackenzie drew a deep, thoughtful breath. "I have some news." He knelt down and grasped her hands in both of his.

"Thank ye fer everything ye've done fer me," he began. "I know it cannae have been easy, and I'm so sorry yer brother was caught up in this whole horrible mess my uncle has created."

"I should be apologising to you," she countered.

"I willnae hear a word of it." Mr Mackenzie squeezed her hands. "But I need ye tae hear this. After ye left, Mr Daniels, yer brother, and I had a conversation."

He stopped, seemingly in thought. The longer he stayed silent, the more Beatrice began to worry. She was just about to ask him what had happened when he spoke again.

"Miss Hartley," he said seriously. "Will ye marry me?"

CHAPTER TWENTY-TWO

Godshollow would be Duncan's.

After Miss Hartley's fight with her brother, Mr Daniels had given Major Hartley some harsh words of his own.

"I am seriously concerned by your behaviour," he'd stated in much calmer tones than Miss Hartley had used. "Why did you not come to me about your financial troubles? If you don't want to admit what the debt is for, so be it, but having debtors getting involved could have had serious repercussions for Godshollow.

"May I remind you that this property is not yours? You do *not* get to decide its future based on *your* circumstances. If anyone was making claims about ownership, I should have been informed as soon as you knew. You have known about Laird Mackenzie for some time now, but you chose not to inform me. That is unacceptable. Truly, I would usually reward such an action with termination of your position as my tenant."

After he paused, Major Hartley smirked at Duncan. Duncan himself felt ill at the idea that the Major would suffer no consequences for his actions.

But Mr Daniels wasn't finished.

"As it is, it doesn't matter who is my tenant anymore. Tomorrow morning I intend to sign over Godshollow to Mr Mackenzie."

Duncan and Major Hartley spoke in unison.

"Really?"

"Yes," Mr Daniels answered. "To be honest, I never wanted this property. I'm happy at home in Oxfordshire. I kept

Godshollow because Annabelle was so enamoured of the place. You know I had plans to sell the property eventually."

He raised his voice to make himself heard over Major Hartley's spluttering.

"I'll pay you for the year you've worked as my tenant, as well as for this year, seeing as you've worked over half of it. I suggest you use the money to re-enlist and buy yourself a commission. Mr Mackenzie will own Godshollow, and something tells me your sister will be well provided for, if you want to pretend any concern on her part."

"Aye, she will," Duncan replied. Mr Daniels had known him for less than a day, but clearly he'd seen the connection between Duncan and Miss Hartley.

That had led Duncan to his current situation of proposing to Miss Hartley.

"Lass, I cannae thank ye enough fer everything ye've done fer me, I really cannae. But I'll settle fer trying everyday tae make ye as happy as ye've made me. Now that I'm getting Godshollow I realise that it willnae be the same without ye. *I* willnae be the same without ye. I want ye here at Godshollow, nae as a tenant, but as it's mistress. Will ye be ma wife and stay here with me?"

His heart was in his mouth as he waited for her reply. She stood silent at first, as though deep in thought, but soon she was wearing the most beautiful smile he had ever seen.

"You don't have to thank me for what I've done," she told him. "I just don't want you to feel that you have to marry me to make us *even*."

"That didnae even cross ma mind, lass. Yer an incredible woman—I've thought so since I met ye. Even when I thought ye were the maid, I knew ye were special. I'd nae ever really given thought tae marrying, but I know I want tae spend the rest of ma life with ye."

"That's what I want too," she replied.

"Is that a yes?"

"Yes," she laughed.

Duncan felt a rush of joy wash through him. He stepped forward and kissed her with all his might. When they broke apart, he kept his arms around her, and she laid her head against his chest.

"I'm not saying yes just because I want to stay at Godshollow," she said in a panic a few moments later.

He chuckled. "I know, lass."

Mr Daniels was suitably congratulatory when he heard of their engagement. Jasper had left Godshollow, no doubt to inform Mr Ocheridge about how spectacularly their plan had failed.

"You deserve the very best," Mr Daniels told Miss Hartley. "And I'm sure Mr Mackenzie will try his very hardest to give it to you."

"Ye have ma word," Duncan replied.

"Then welcome to the family, sir."

They toasted with a drink, and Duncan spent the evening getting to know Mr Daniels better. He explained the basics of his family situation, and in return was told about the reason Mr Daniels was alone.

"She really wanted yer niece tae be together with the Welshman so much?" he asked in disbelief.

"She did," Mr Daniels confirmed. "I had no choice."

"Incredible!"

"Indeed."

"Has she written to you recently," Miss Hartley asked curiously.

"Not that I'm aware of, though I will probably go home to a dozen waiting for me. At this point in time, it is still the best option for us."

Duncan, meanwhile, was thinking about a different part of the story. "Mrs Lutton is certainly a formidable woman. Not many other women of her age would stand against a man in that situation."

"She is one of a kind," Mr Daniels joked. "And you will be seeing a lot of her when you move in here properly. Which reminds me, Miss Hartley, you must inform her of your engagement. She'll be overjoyed."

Miss Hartley laughed. "You know she'll take all the credit, of course. She worked very hard to make that ball as romantic for us as possible. I think she fancies herself the best matchmaker this side of London."

"Ach, Lord," Duncan exclaimed. "She isnae going tae expect us tae name our first child after her, is she?" His words were said in jest, but Duncan did have real underlying concern. She was a strong-willed woman.

"I'm certain of it," Miss Hartley assured him teasingly.

"Lord help us."

CHAPTER TWENTY-THREE

When the group gathered for breakfast the next morning, Jasper was still absent. Beatrice wasn't impressed, but she wasn't surprised. He wasn't getting his own way, so he was sulking. Recent events had forced her to consider her relationship with her brother. The more she did, the more negative she felt.

But that wasn't the important issue at that point. Today was about Mr Mackenzie. She was full of nervous energy. Mr Mackenzie's dream was so close to coming true, and that meant all the secrets were going to come out. The confrontations weren't going to be pleasant, but it would be very satisfying to see Laird Mackenzie's plans ruined, and his hold over Mr Mackenzie destroyed.

Mr Mackenzie, too, was that volatile mix of excitement and anxiety.'

Mr Daniels, on the other hand, was a picture of serenity. He hummed happily as he ate and had an air of quiet dignity. Perhaps it was a military tactic. Pretending to be happy could trick one's mind into thinking one was enjoying the prospect of going into battle. That, or Mr Daniels was more likely just the kind of person who didn't let things faze him easily.

"Shall we be off?" he suggested cheerily.

Mr Daniels felt that if they approached Mr Ocheridge to legalise the documents, that would be a fitting punishment for him. He would refuse, of course, which meant he would suffer the further injury of watching his partner, Mr Widdersham, pocket the legal fees for the work.

Beatrice and Mr Mackenzie followed Mr Daniels's lead when they reached the offices in town, just under an hour after they left Godshollow.

Mr Daniels banged the heavy brass knocker on the door. Just as he went to knock it again, three minutes later, they were greeted once again by the unhappy maid.

"Is it urgent?" she asked testily.

"Yes," Mr Daniels informed her. "We have business to discuss with Messrs. Ocheridge and Widdersham."

"Can't it wait?" she replied tiredly. "Mr Ocheridge isn't in the best of moods this mornin'. Couldn't Mr Widdersham handle it on 'is own?"

"We need both of them," Mr Daniels pressed.

She didn't move. This time, Beatrice dealt with the lady.

"I'm terribly sorry you had to deal with that. I'm afraid in all likelihood, he won't be best pleased with what we have to say." She reached into her reticule and pulled out some coins. "If you could just let us in, you can go to get some breakfast, if you like. There was a lovely little pub I saw on the way in."

The maid eyed the coins, staring at them like she was being offered the crown jewels.

"Fine," she said begrudgingly.

She left the three of them standing on the doorstep. They exchanged unimpressed glances.

A little while later, the woman came back and ushered them in. "He says you can wait for him upstairs and he'll see you with Mr Widdersham when he's ready." Then she held her hand out for the coins. Beatrice obliged, and the woman fled the house like a thief leaving an art gallery.

"That was a promising start," Mr Daniels remarked drily as they mounted the stairs.

"That poor woman," Beatrice worried. "I hadn't considered the ramifications of Mr Ocheridge's temper. Are we sure this is a good idea?"

"It has to be done," Mr Daniels lamented. "Hopefully, she's been wise enough to take the money and just leave. I saw how much you gave her."

"She knew what tae do," Mr Mackenzie added. "The issue here is how long do ye think he'll keep us waiting?"

An hour.

An hour was how long he kept them waiting, and Beatrice was bored out of her mind. There were no books in the sitting room, and the view was no better from any side of the house, not just from the one looking out over the wild park.

Mr Mackenzie had started pacing about thirty minutes into their wait, and even Mr Daniels was beginning to look irritated.

Finally, Mr Ocheridge graced them with his presence. He was followed out of his office by Jasper, who didn't say anything to the trio as he left and avoided meeting any of their gazes.

"Are you ready to begin?" Ocheridge asked. No greeting. No apology for the wait. And no Widdersham.

"Will your partner be joining us?" Mr Daniels asked forcefully.

"We don't really need to get him involved, do we?" Mr Ocheridge asked nervously.

"Aye, we do," Mr Mackenzie asserted.

"He isn't ready."

"We've waited this long," Beatrice countered. "We can do it a little longer."

With an exasperated huff, Ocheridge went to find Widdersham, who, contrary to his assertions, was more than ready and came out presently.

Nobody said anything and they followed Mr Ocheridge into his office.

The room was a mess. It looked worse than if a hurricane

had blown through. He must have been very angry indeed when Jasper explained everything to him.

As she looked around the chaotic room, Beatrice noticed that Ocheridge had only put out two visitor chairs. Even now, he was still trying to exclude her. His plan, however, was foiled when Mr Widdersham followed them in.

"Good lord, Ocheridge. What happened in here? We'd best use my office, I think. When Miriam said you were in a bad mood this morning, I'd assumed you were just being grumpy."

The group moved into Widdersham's office, which was much tidier. Although sadly suffering from the same limitations the building itself imposed, being small and slightly cramped, it was certainly much neater and better organised than Mr Ocheridge's.

There were enough seats for everyone. Beatrice delighted in taking the seat directly opposite Mr Ocheridge.

"I take it, Miss Hartley, you are here for a marriage license." Mr Widdersham addressed Beatrice, much to her surprise.

Mr Mackenzie was just as bewildered. "How do ye know about the engagement?" he asked suspiciously.

"I met Miss Hartley only the other day."

"We were only engaged last night," Mr Mackenzie argued.

"What?" Mr Ocheridge baulked. Beatrice had wondered if he was going to say something—if he was going to fight for the sham engagement between them even, though Jasper had presumably told him the truth.

"Would you like to explain, Mr Ocheridge? Or shall we?" Beatrice found an interesting pleasure in watching Ocheridge squirm. Eventually, through gritted teeth, he begrudgingly answered.

"My and Miss Hartley's engagement was . . ." He paused. Beatrice wondered if he would actually admit the lie. " . . .

terminated."

She could only laugh. "You're absolutely incredible," she said incredulously.

"Just what exactly is going on here?" Mr Widdersham demanded.

"This is absurd," Mr Ocheridge said. "Just sign the damn papers and go."

"Dunnae ye think Mr Widdersham should know what kind of a man his partner is?" Mr Mackenzie asked.

"I will not stand here and listen to . . . to slander." He stood, as if he intended to leave the office.

"Stay right where you are." Mr Daniels had seemed happy to observe thus far, but he was adding his measured command into the situation now.

"Just what the bloody hell is going on?" Mr Widdersham demanded in exasperation.

"A very good question," Mr Daniels said calmly, bringing out the collection of documents they had and laying them on the table. "I think these papers might explain a few things. Your partner here has been involved in some questionable dealings. You may be aware that Mr Mackenzie here was falsely imprisoned for theft. Pay close attention to this section of the letter here." He pointed at a certain passage. "It says *by whatever means necessary.*"

And so Widdersham was apprised of everything that had brought them all to the point they had reached. It was amusing at first to see Ocheridge try to defend his behaviour, but soon his actions simply became offensive as he pulled out lie after lie and hurled baseless accusations with abandon.

Naturally, Mr Widdersham tried to side with his colleague, but he found it hard to deny the evidence.

"It's inadmissible," Ocheridge shrieked. "That's my private property, and you've stolen it."

"It is damning," Mr Widdersham admitted. "Though he

has a point. How did you come by this?"

Beatrice looked to her companions and they exchanged worried glances.

"It was me," she admitted at length, much to the other's disapproval, judging by their frowns. "I knew something wasn't right. Mr Ocheridge and my brother were lying to me, and they were putting Mr Mackenzie's life at risk with false accusations. I had to do something. Is it really stealing if the papers were stolen in the first place?"

"What were they lying about?" Mr Widdersham probed.

"They were taking advantage of a head injury to try and manipulate me into believing their version of events, including an engagement that I never consented to."

Ocheridge was now as pale as fresh milk and had ceased his useless defence.

Mr Widdersham put the papers down and sat in thoughtful silence. Nobody seemed to want to be the one to break his process, so they were all quiet.

Beatrice watched him, wondering what on earth was going through his mind at that moment.

"This is a lot of information to process at once," Widdersham said at length. "I think it will take some time for me to fully accept everything that has happened. That being said, I am utterly appalled. Ocheridge" — he turned to his partner — "your actions have been despicable. I'm disappointed in you, but also in myself for not having any knowledge of your actions. I thought you were a man I could trust. I'm going to have to ask you to leave."

There was nothing more that Ocheridge could do. Beatrice took great satisfaction in watching him slink away, tail between his legs.

Widdersham then turned to the three who remained.

"Mr Mackenzie, I can only apologise for the way you have been treated. Whether you or your uncle has the greater claim to Godshollow is not my concern. Your case should never have been handled that way. I can only be sorry that your case was found by Ocheridge and not by myself."

Beatrice reached over to Mr Mackenzie and took his hand, giving him a supportive squeeze as the man thanked Mr Widdersham for his apology.

"Unfortunately, not knowing your case well, I can't even begin to advise on who owns Godshollow or who should own it."

"Quite understandable," Mr Daniels put in. "With regards to that, Mr Mackenzie and myself have come to an agreement. We simply need you to draft the papers and officiate."

Widdersham agreed, and despite Mr Daniels's protests that none of it was Widdersham's fault, he offered to do the work for free as compensation.

"I need it to be infallible," Mr Daniels explained. "I do not give Godshollow to the Mackenzie family as a whole. I want the paperwork to be for Duncan Mackenzie alone, and his wife when they are married. His father was the eldest brother in line for the entailment, so that means it goes to his son."

"Are you sure that's what you want to do?" Mr Widdersham asked. "Even if the claim were unenforceable?"

"Yes. I planned on selling it eventually, and really, I'm of no age to be dealing with a sale. I've earned enough already for a comfortable life. Mr Mackenzie is much more deserving of the opportunities this could bring a man."

"That's very generous."

"The last few years have given me a better perspective of what's important. And anyway, I think that giving away a property because of old ownership is much better than losing a property playing cards."

Mr Daniels had a twinkle in his eye that Beatrice had seen so many times in his niece, Annabelle, whenever she was doing something that made someone else happy.

Within an hour, the papers had been drawn up and signed. Godshollow officially belonged to Mr Mackenzie.

They parted from Mr Widdersham with a friendly handshake and mutual apologies for either party having to go through, or discover, what had gone on in the last months.

On the street outside the law office, they celebrated loudly. There was no sign of Mr Ocheridge, who, if he had any sense, would be embarking on a life in hiding. Beatrice certainly wouldn't have minded never seeing the man again.

Mr Mackenzie couldn't stop thanking Mr Daniels and marvelling at his new home.

"Ma nanna would be so happy," he commented a little way into their journey.

Beatrice squeezed his hand. "I wish I could have met her," she responded in complete honesty. Caitlín Mackenzie sounded like a remarkable woman, full of love and caring, with a strong streak of confidence and good sense.

Mr Mackenzie reached into his jacket pocket and pulled out a little frame that held two miniatures. He held them out to Beatrice.

"Is that her?" Beatrice asked, her fingers ghosting over the picture. The woman had a cheery, round face with bright brown eyes and deep brown hair. Next to that picture was a man. He looked almost like Mr Mackenzie but not quite. The man had the same hair and eyes, though his face was more angular, and his shoulders weren't as broad.

"Aye, lass. That's her." His voice had a tone of pride and adoration in it.

"You look a lot like her," Beatrice commented, taking the frame from his hand and examining it.

"Do I?" Mr Mackenzie asked. He was smiling.

"Yes, you have the same eyes. And your ears have the same dainty point at the top."

Mr Mackenzie ran a finger along the curve of his ear. "I

havenae ever noticed that."

"It's true," Beatrice asserted. "But you have your father's nose. That is your father, isn't it?"

"Aye," he confirmed. He paused. "Ye know, I think he was about ma age when that miniature was done."

"Really? He looks older somehow."

Mr Mackenzie laughed. "Nanna always said he was old before his time. He worried a lot."

"My mother was the same," Beatrice reminisced. "She was always so worried about everyone else. She took on so much guilt she didn't have to. My father was always trying to convince her to relax."

They were nearing Godshollow. Mr Mackenzie became quiet and watched intently from the carriage window.

His gaze was fixed on the towers peeking from the trees.

"What are you thinking about?" Beatrice asked him softly.

"I own those towers," he commented in awe. "I'm the owner of Godshollow." He looked apprehensive and nervous. "Fer a while, I didnae think I'd ever get this chance."

"But you did, and you are," Beatrice assured him, grasping his hand. "This is happening."

"This can't be happening!"

Beatrice stood with her fiancé in the courtyard of the property and a man in a tartan kilt, with small, beady eyes, and a hard mouth was standing at the door.

"I'm afraid I'm gonnae have tae ask ye tae leave ma property."

CHAPTER TWENTY-FOUR

"This is absurd." Duncan couldn't believe what was happening. His uncle was at Godshollow. Not only that, he was at Godshollow claiming it as his own.

"*I* am the owner of this property." Duncan told Graeme Mackenzie defiantly. "I decide who is allowed in or nae."

"I'm afraid yer mistaken, Duncan."

Graeme was striding towards them, waving to them like some despotic monarch, cigar casually held in one hand. Duncan could just about see his mother standing back by the door, watching on with worry.

"Ye cannae do this.," Duncan challenged. "This is ma home. Get out." He wasn't going to play any of this man's games.

Graeme tutted. "That is nae way tae speak tae yer family. Yer only uncle," he chided.

Duncan laughed. "That's how ye treated me," he shouted back. "Ye denied I even was yer family."

"True," Graeme replied with a smirk. "And in that case, I'm really gonnae have tae ask ye tae leave. Godshollow belongs tae the Mackenzies. And ye arenae a Mackenzie."

"This castle belongs tae me." Duncan held aloft the paper he'd signed not hours ago. "What are ye even doing here?"

"I'm only fulfilling ma dear mother's dying wish tae see this castle in our family's hands again."

Duncan was so angry he thought he was going to be sick. But for once, he was facing his uncle without fear. He wasn't scared of him anymore. He was just angry.

"Dunnae act like ye ever cared about her," he bit back.

Graeme laughed. "So ye've finally started tae be a man?" his uncle asked condescendingly. "Standing up fer yerself at last? Ye were always such a timid wee mouse."

Duncan was surprised, though he supposed he shouldn't be, when Miss Hartley spoke up in his defense.

"He's more brave and good than you'll ever be," she said defiantly.

"This isnae yer concern, lass," Graeme warned.

"It is very much my concern," she contradicted. She had moved forward and was standing directly in front of Graeme. She was edging closer and closer, to within touching distance.

Duncan put a hand on her shoulder.

"Miss Hartley is ma fiancée. She has far more right tae care about this place than ye have."

"Fiancée?" This time his uncle was actually surprised.

Duncan grinned. *That's right. I've found someone tae love me. I amnae the repulsive, unlovable creature ye tried tae tell me I was.*

Graeme schooled his features back to neutrality. "That may be so, but ye still cannae come in," he stated.

"But I've got the deeds," Duncan countered. "Ye cannae stop me."

Graeme smiled. He turned on his heel and strode towards the front doors. Opening them, he revealed a line of men. They were wearing redcoats, and each one carried a rifle.

"Leave *ma* property or I'll be forced tae let them shoot ye."

For a second, Duncan considered just walking up to the men, testing his uncle's resolve. But then he remembered the patron of the inn who'd tried to dispute what he owed. His uncle had threatened to shoot him if he didn't pay. The man's body had been carried out by his friends.

"Ye cannae just board yerself up in there, ye madman," Duncan shouted to him.

"I can do what I like in ma home," Graeme replied.

"It's *not* your home," Miss Hartley cried. "You can't do

this."

Duncan thought she was having the same thoughts he'd had seconds ago. He grabbed her arm and pulled her away.

"Dunnae try him, lass. He *will* tell them tae shoot ye."

"You have ten seconds tae leave," Graeme yelled.

Duncan took him at his word. All but dragging Miss Hartley and leading Mr Daniels back to the carriage, Duncan explained his uncle's previous behaviour.

"That man wasnae the first and willnae be the last ma uncle destroys fer his own ends. We should go somewhere safe tae come up with a plan."

He felt as if they were running away as he climbed into the carriage, but they were simply rallying. Fighting Graeme without a method of doing so would be stupid. He instructed the driver to get them out of Godshollow as quickly as possible.

"This is unbelievable," Miss Hartley said in exasperation. Duncan wrapped an arm around her shoulders.

"We need a plan," Mr Daniels asserted rather superfluously. "We've got to get him out here so you can get in."

"I'd take a guess and say all the entrances are being guarded," Miss Hartley surmised. "That's the first thing I'd do."

"We cannae start a war of attrition with him. We cannae win. We wait fer him tae leave. We go in. They wait fer us tae leave. They go in. There isnae an end. I cannae live ma life waiting fer Graeme tae strike. We need tae get the magistrate there with us."

"But he won't come out," Miss Hartley pointed out. "Even if we get the magistrate here, what could he do, really? From what you've told me, your uncle won't go peacefully."

"Yer right. He willnae give up just because someone says he has tae leave. I need tae get in there tae force him out when the magistrate arrives."

"That could be extremely dangerous," Mr Daniels put in. "You're most certainly going to get hurt."

"Rather me than someone else," Duncan replied. "It's time ma uncle was stopped. I'm going tae be the one tae stop him. I have tae face him."

Duncan could see that Mr Daniels was still concerned about the plan, but something in him respected Duncan's sense of duty and need for closure.

"You know him better than I do," Mr Daniels conceded. "I can only advise you. I do think you'd be putting yourself at risk, but I can't stop you."

"Thank ye."

Mr Daniels gave him a quick nod. "I do have one question though. How will you get in?"

Duncan didn't have an immediate answer. Odds were that his uncle had all entrances secured with his men.

"We need to go to Mrs Lutton," Miss Hartley said decisively when Duncan stayed silent. "We can talk through our options somewhere warm, and the General can help us with the Redcoats."

"A decent suggestion," Mr Daniels admitted.

"But that will all take too long," Duncan countered. "The longer we leave him there, the longer he has tae entrench himself."

"We need time to think," Miss Hartley retorted. "And any extra help will be invaluable."

He had to admit she was right. They needed reinforcements. He just wasn't sure if an elderly couple, however active and willing they were, would be of much help.

He watched Godshollow fade away into the distance. He'd been so close — he couldn't lose now.

"What I want to know," Mr Daniels put in, "is where did your uncle even get that many men? Did he bring them from Scotland?"

"Nae," Duncan replied.

Miss Hartley went pale. "I think I know," she admitted. Her tone sounded as though her words caused her pain. "Jasper. He still has connections in the army. He could have convinced them." She put her head in her hands. "I can't believe this."

Duncan wanted to comfort her, but what could he say? This maddening situation had, in part, been brought about by her brother. That was undeniable.

"I'm sorry, lass. But it isnae over yet."

After maybe ten minutes of fast travel, the carriage came to a sudden stop. Duncan got out. He realised he hadn't given the driver any directions other than to get away from the castle.

But it wasn't the driver who had caused them to stop. In the middle of the road stood Major Hartley. Duncan had half a mind to order the driver to just keep going and run the Major over if he refused to get out of the way. But Miss Hartley, as much as she didn't like her brother at that moment, wouldn't be happy if they killed him.

"What do ye want?" Duncan asked shortly.

The Major looked humbled and contrite. "I want to help you."

That took Duncan by surprise. He just stood and stared at the other man.

"What do ye mean ye want tae help? Dunnae ye think ye've done enough already?"

Major Hartley was going to say something, but he was interrupted.

"What's going on?" Miss Hartley had gotten out of the carriage to discover the source of the delay. When she saw her brother, her expression grew cold.

"What are you doing here?"

Major Hartley took a step back when Miss Hartley fixed

him with a hard stare.

"I have a way for you to get into the castle."

"Why should we believe you?" Miss Hartley demanded harshly.

"I was just doing what I thought was best for us. The money would have helped us. And I thought being useful to the potential owner would be beneficial."

"But that's just the problem, Jasper. *I.I.I.* You did it all without a word to me or to Mr Daniels. You decided that *you* knew best. None of what you did was worth security. I'd rather live in poverty with a brother I loved than to live in style with a man I couldn't stand to look at."

Duncan actually felt a little sorry for the Major. He looked wounded.

"Why do ye want tae help us now?" he asked.

"I want to prove I only acted from desperation, not malice."

"That's not good enough." Miss Hartley was not convinced.

"Well, then . . ." Major Hartley took a deep breath. "Let me help you to start making reparations for what I've done."

Duncan looked to Miss Hartley. She was wary, but there was a small glimmer of hope in her eyes.

"What's yer way in?" he asked the Major.

"There's a hidden entrance," Major Hartley explained. "That's where your uncle said Ocheridge would find the original deed. Hidden behind a bookcase. There was a tunnel—"

"Aye." Duncan cut across him with realisation. "Lady Mackenzie escaped the siege through a tunnel. Do ye know where it comes out?"

"Follow me," the Major instructed.

"Could somebody tell me what's going on, please. I thought we were going to Mrs Lutton's home."

Mr Daniels had poked his head out of the carriage window.

"I think I might have a way intae Godshollow," Duncan replied tentatively.

"Mr Daniels, *yer* going tae go tae the Luttons with Miss Hartley as she suggested."

"And what are you going to do? How on earth could you get in?"

"*I* am going tae go fer a walk with the Major here."

"Are you sure about that?"

"He did tell the truth," Duncan admitted. "He gave useful information that he didnae have tae."

Mr Daniels begrudgingly acquiesced and disappeared back into the carriage. Miss Hartley, however, wasn't as obliging. "Don't think for a moment I'm letting you go alone."

Duncan sighed. Of course she wanted to come with him She had that adventurer's spirit that he admired so greatly. But that course of action wasn't safe.

"Nae."

Major Hartley also felt confident enough to voice his disagreement. "That is not an idea that is up for discussion."

Miss Hartley first turned to her brother.

"Don't you dare assume you can tell me what to do," she snapped. When she spoke to Duncan, her tone was softer but still firm.

"I'm coming with you."

"There's nae time tae argue, lass. It's far too dangerous fer ye tae come with me. Ma uncle's already threatened tae shoot us. I willnae put ye in harm's way. He could seriously hurt ye."

"I'm not letting you go in on your own."

"It's best if I go alone. I wasnae even gonnae ask yer brother tae help."

"Why not?" she demanded. "He owes you."

"Because yer brother is gonnae talk tae the soldiers."

"I am?" Major Hartley paused. "Oh yes, I am."

"Then you definitely need to take me with you," Miss Hartley protested. "I know the inside of Godshollow better than you do. Who knows where we'll come out of a secret tunnel? I've got a much better chance of finding the main staircase and wherever your uncle might be."

"All right, lass," Duncan conceded begrudgingly. "But if I tell ye tae run or tae hide, ye *do* it. No argument."

Miss Hartley consented to his terms, although Duncan knew she had no intention of following his orders. But then, he wouldn't have her any other way.

Mr Daniels was about as pleased with the idea of Miss Hartley going as Duncan was. Like him, he was powerless to stop her doing what she wanted.

"Please be careful," he appealed to her as he prepared to leave. "If it's a choice between yourself and Godshollow, you know which one I'd pick."

"Thank you," she replied sincerely. "But that decision won't have to be made."

He didn't look convinced, but Duncan promised him he'd look after her, and Mr Daniels left to inform the Luttons and the magistrate of what was transpiring.

"Lead on, Jasper," Miss Hartley instructed. Her tone was short and sharp. She sounded nowhere near ready to trust her brother so soon after his perfidy. As much harm as the Major had done to Duncan, he hated to see Miss Hartley's relationship with her brother break. He suspected they'd never had the best of times, but this was far worse than anything they'd been through. This had changed them forever, but Duncan hoped she wouldn't lose someone she loved.

They followed Major Hartley, leaving the road, going in a fairly straight line as the woods gave way to more open landscape, though the route was still littered with wild bushes and shrubs that stretched out like a natural boundary line.

They walked for so long that Duncan was worried they

were never going to find this tunnel entrance. He tried to push down the worry that the Major might be leading them into a trap. But it was too late to go back.

Finally, his trust was rewarded. The landscape had changed, with the land to the left of them beginning to rise until the slope of the ground was taller than Duncan.

"There it is!" Miss Hartley cried out. Duncan couldn't be certain if she was happier they'd found a way in, or that Major Hartley hadn't been lying to them.

Miss Hartley increased her pace, making for a gap in the slope. A large part of the earth had been cut away, revealing the entrance.

"When I followed the tunnel, it came out here," Major Hartley explained. "The entrance was overgrown with weeds and brambles, so it was tricky getting through."

There was indeed evidence of that. Thick roots and vines had clearly been disturbed. Some were broken, others merely bent out of shape. Thinking how it must have looked before, Duncan wasn't surprised that more people hadn't found it before now.

The door also showed signs of age and deterioration. The metal fastenings were rusted into place, and years of English weather had warped the bottom of the wooden panels. Duncan had to pull hard, but eventually he forced the door open.

Inside, a basic tunnel was revealed, narrow and low, with wooden supports at regular intervals to reinforce the hollowed-out area and protect the tunnel from collapse. The dirt floor proceeded straight into darkness.

"Are ye sure ye want tae come with me, lass?" Duncan asked, giving her one last opportunity to head to safety.

Miss Hartley replied with a look that let him know exactly what she thought of that question. But before she joined Duncan at the mouth of the tunnel, she turned to her brother.

"Go to the courtyard and try to occupy the soldiers. Get

them to leave, if you can," she told him. Her tone was still forthright and unfriendly. But she softened a little. "I can't forgive what you've done. I know you have your reasons, but I'm not ready yet. Though this has helped."

"Be careful," he replied. He turned and started back the way they'd come.

Miss Hartley joined Duncan by the door.

"Ready?" she asked.

Chapter Twenty-Five

The tunnel was cold, dark, and damp, much as a tunnel should be. Beatrice wasn't sure why she'd expected anything different. A dirty, dusty smell dominated her senses as the light disappeared.

She called out to Mr Mackenzie to assure herself he was with her. In the darkness, she couldn't see past the end of her own nose.

"I'm here, lass."

His voice was closer than she'd expected, and she jumped.

"I cannae see a thing. How are we supposed tae find our way?"

"We need to get candles or a lamp," Beatrice replied.

"We havenae the time. Ma uncle needs tae be stopped now."

"Then we'll just have to feel the walls and follow it that way."

She put her arms out wearily. Apparently, Mr Mackenzie had done the same, because his hand soon found hers.

"Hold onto me. I don't believe there are multiple tunnels, but I'd hate for us to lose each other." She was trying to sound confident, but she was full of apprehension. She couldn't know what they were heading into and she wanted to help, but she couldn't deny she *was* scared. In this situation, anyone who wasn't scared to be in her position seriously needed to take a look at themselves.

"Yer doing fine, lass," Mr Mackenzie encouraged her. "We'll be out of here soon."

"That's what I'm worried about."

"I cannae say it'll all be fine, but yer the strongest woman I know. I wouldnae want anyone else tae be by ma side right now." He paused to wrap her in a hug. As he leant his chin on the top of her head, he tensed.

"Wh—?" Beatrice began before he shushed her.

"Can ye hear that?" he asked quietly.

She strained to figure out what he was hearing. A low, rhythmic noise, as if someone was singing. But the sound didn't seem to be coming from the tunnel.

"We must be inside Godshollow," he told her in a whisper. "I can hear someone."

"Yes!" she exclaimed. But she immediately quieted down. "We can't have much farther to go."

True enough, the floor of the corridor began to rise at a sharper incline, and soon they were facing a dead-end. A faint beam of light followed the vertical line of the wall.

Beatrice felt along the line.

"It's wood," she announced.

Mr Mackenzie began searching to her left. "Is there a handle? We've got tae find the way tae open it."

There wasn't a handle, so Beatrice's first attempt was to push against the wood. It wouldn't budge.

"What did the story say?" she asked Mr Mackenzie. "How did they open it?"

"It was done from the other side. There was a lever hidden behind a painting."

"Then there's got to be a way to work it from this side."

They worked in silence, feeling in the dark to find a way to open the door.

Beatrice focussed on the space level with her shoulders and above. If the level on the other side was behind a painting, it was going to be higher up. Eventually, she felt something different under her fingertips—a small, circular metal lump. As she probed, she felt it move backwards, followed be a soft click as the beam of light from the door grew thicker.

"Was that it?" she asked excitedly.

Mr Mackenzie quietly shushed her and moved towards the opening. Beatrice didn't realise she was holding her breath until she let it out when Mr Mackenzie spoke.

"I cannae hear anyone." He kept his voice quiet and low, and gingerly moved the wooden door wider. "There isnae anyone in the room."

"We should be able to get in without being seen," she agreed.

"Are ye sure ye still want tae do this?" he asked. Beatrice was sure he knew what the answer would be, but it was kind of him to offer her a way out just once more.

"I've made it this far," she joked.

She gently pushed the door and prayed they hadn't just alerted anyone to their presence. There might not have been anyone in the room to witness them coming out of the wall, but there could be any number of soldiers, or even Duncan's uncle, just outside in the hall.

They slowly emerged into a small library. Beatrice ran to the window, but stayed low, not wanting to give them away if she was seen. She was trying to figure out where exactly in Godshollow this was.

From her view, she estimated they were in the west wing, on the third floor under the attic.

"What can ye see?" Mr Mackenzie asked.

"I know where we are," she answered. "We just need to find out where your uncle is."

"Where do we even start?"

That was a good question. They couldn't openly walk through the house checking every room. They had no idea how many men Mackenzie had, or what they'd been instructed to do if they saw either of them.

They needed a way to move about that carried minimal risk of being seen.

"There weren't any other secret tunnels your nanna mentioned?" Beatrice was only half joking. More hidden passageways would really help.

"Nae," Mr Mackenzie answered sadly. He stood motionless, deep in thought. "Does Godshollow have separate servant's stairs? We had them as a way of staying out of the way of customers at the inn."

Beatrice could see what he was thinking and had been thinking along similar lines herself. It was their best chance, provided the other Mr Mackenzie didn't consider the servants or their means of going about the castle.

This prompted Beatrice to realise she hadn't even considered the staff and what had happened to them when Mr Mackenzie's uncle had arrived. She felt incredibly guilty that she hadn't thought about Mr Peters or anyone else, but she hoped she would find them safe and well.

After checking that the hallway was empty, Beatrice led Mr Mackenzie towards the back of the house to the servant's passageways. The old wooden staircase was thankfully empty, but as they descended, they could hear more people. Voices could be heard in the hall, and they were getting louder. Mr Mackenzie pulled Beatrice and pressed them both against the wall next to the door. The men were now so close that she and Mr Mackenzie could clearly hear what they were saying.

"Do we have any idea what all of this is about?" one man asked.

"What does it matter?" a second man replied. "Captain Harding said we've been promised a lot of money to do this. Rumour is this Ocheridge gent is a lawyer—they're fairly flush in the pocket, right? And if all I have to do is walk up and down a hallway and shoot any Scotsman other than the laird who appears, then all the better."

"I know, but I had plans this week with the missus. She was right angry when I told her I had to go."

Beatrice held her breath as the men outside moved even closer. Mr Mackenzie had balled his hands into fists, no doubt expecting a fight.

The voices were on the other side of the door now. "Shall we check?"

"All the servants are cooped up in the kitchen. Henderson's watching them. Nobody will have gotten in there in the thirty minutes since we last checked."

"You're probably right. Let's go back to the stairwell and report."

The voices began to recede as the men walked back down the corridor. Beatrice was able to get some much-needed air into her burning lungs.

"That was too close," Mr Mackenzie hissed.

"We can't stay in here forever. We need to get to the kitchens. Mr Peters might know where your uncle is. No doubt he's picked a room to run things from."

Beatrice bit her lip thoughtfully. "You should stay with Mr Peters when we find him." Mr Mackenzie started to argue but she cut him off. "You heard what they said. They have orders to shoot any Scotsman they find."

"Then I willae say anything."

"And what, the kilt is just a fashion choice?"

He looked down at himself, and his smirk faded.

Anxiety coiled itself around Beatrice's soul and gripped her tight.

"I willnae let ye go alone."

Beatrice rubbed her face and took a long breath. "Fine. But if you get shot, I *will* be telling you I was right."

"I dunnae think I'd be in a state tae argue with ye." His tone was light and joking but touched on a truth that terrified her.

"Let's just get to the kitchen," she said, trying to push down the rising fear.

They descended the servant's stairs until they could hear them talking.

Beatrice opened the service door just a little, trying to see what they could be walking into.

Mr Peters, Tobias, her maid Sophie, the cook Mrs Wethering, and the scullery maid Tiffany were sitting around a table. The soldier who was supposed to be guarding them, according to the men they'd overheard earlier, wasn't there.

She opened the door a little farther. This caught Tobias's attention, and the young lad hurried over to her. He spoke quietly, so Beatrice assumed the soldier wasn't too far away. They had to be quick.

"What're you doing here, Miss?" Toby asked in concern. His eyes went wide when he saw Mr Mackenzie behind her.

"You shouldn't be here," the boy cautioned. "I heard them. They want to hurt him." Tobias's behaviour had brought Mr Peters, who didn't look happy to see them.

"We know," Beatrice confirmed. "But we have to do something. Mr Daniels is getting the magistrate. We're here to force Mackenzie to concede. Do you know where he is?"

Mr Peters clearly didn't like what their questions suggested, but he gave them the information they wanted.

"He's in the study on the first-floor, so said Sophie. That's where they made you take the food, isn't it?" He'd turned to the maid who nodded her head fearfully.

"What can we do?" Toby piped up, apparently eager for a fight.

"Stay here," Mr Mackenzie said over the top of Beatrice's head. "Dunnae give them any reason tae think there's anything suspicious happening." He paused. "Do ye know how many men he has?"

"About a dozen," Mr Peters replied.

"Two of them we've already passed," Beatrice said counting them off on her fingers. "One of them is here with you."

"He's talking to another one," Toby added helpfully.

"That leaves eight," Mr Mackenzie summarised.

"Some must be guarding the door."

"Aye. And some will be by the study."

Mr Peters had wandered away during their counting of the soldiers and came back with a pair of breeches. Handing them to Mr Mackenzie he said, "Put those on. They know to look for Scotsmen."

Tobias suddenly stood stock still and held up a hand.

"The guard's coming back," he warned in a rushed whisper.

Beatrice nodded and ducked back into the stairwell, closing the door behind her as quietly as she could. She could hear the soldier return, telling the servants to stop moving around and stay at the table as he had ordered. She let out a sigh. The soldier clearly didn't suspect anything. She wondered with foreboding when their luck was going to run out.

Mr Mackenzie tapped her shoulder. "Let's go," he said. He'd changed into the clothes Mr Peters had given him and hidden his kilt under the stairwell.

Beatrice drew a deep breath, squared her shoulders and followed him.

They arrived on the first floor via the servants' stairs without encountering any other people, and Beatrice was feeling good about their plan until they reached the corner to the corridor containing the study Mr Peters had said Mr Mackenzie's uncle was using.

Four scarlet-coated men guarded the door with long, threatening-looking rifles. There was no way she or Mr Mackenzie could get in without being seen and questioned. They'd be found out for sure, and who knew what they'd do to Mr Mackenzie.

She turned to him with concern.

"Ye've done yer job, lass. Go back and let Mr Peters and the others out of the kitchens. I'll deal with ma uncle."

He held her gaze with steady eyes, a soul-searching look that left her feeling breathless. Then he gave her a gentle kiss. She lifted her hands to grasp him, but he stepped away. He put a finger to his lips, telling her to stay quiet, and it was too late when she realised he was stepping into the hallway in full view of the guards.

CHAPTER TWENTY-SIX

Duncan kissed Miss Hartley gently and hoped that she would do as he asked. Then he stepped out into to hallway.

He held his breath as he waited for the soldiers to notice him. That didn't take long. Within seconds, four pairs of eyes were fixed on him, displaying reactions from confusion to suspicion. The muzzle of two rifles were lifted to focus on him.

He opened his mouth, ready to give away his nationality, when there was a shout from behind him. Another soldier had seen Miss Hartley and was trying to get her up on her feet. There was a fight, but Miss Hartley was giving her all. Duncan's priority had to be getting to his uncle.

He tried to take advantage of the confusion to push his way past the men. Shoulder forward, he barrelled into the group of soldiers, but that was an exercise in futility. He wasn't able to reach the door before he was hit with the butt of a gun. He sank to his knees, the wind knocked out of him. When he struggled to regain his feet, hands pushed on his shoulders and kept him down.

"Leave him alone."

He turned his head and saw Miss Hartley. She'd escaped the grasp of the other solider and was rushing down the corridor. "*Stop.*" She tried to push the men away from him, but it didn't take much strength for a guard to lift her off her feet and move her. She did kick and fight, but the soldier was just too big.

The guarded door was opened.

"What's going on out here?"

Graeme stood in the doorway, looming and imposing. He sneered down at Duncan.

"I'm impressed. I thought ye were too white-livered tae try anything. Though I have tae wonder if ye've got more guts than brains. Ye must know ye cannae win."

He turned to the soldiers. "Bring them in here. And give me that." He snatched a rifle out of the hands of one of the soldiers.

Duncan and Miss Hartley were strong-armed by the soldiers into the study.

"Leave us," Graeme commanded.

When it was just the three of them, Duncan moved so that he was between Miss Hartley and his uncle.

Only once he was facing his uncle did he realise he hadn't really thought about what would happen if they got this far. In that moment, all he cared about was that Graeme didn't hurt Miss Hartley.

"Let Miss Hartley leave," he demanded. "This isnae her fight."

"And yet she's here," Graeme countered.

Miss Hartley stepped out from behind Duncan, much to his dismay.

"I am," she confirmed. "You're not going to win."

Graeme laughed, cocked the rifle, then laid the weapon on the desk, and casually lit a cigar he took from an ornate silver box in was a show of power. He was as calm as anything, which only served to fuel Duncan's rage. "Really, lad? Still hiding behind a woman's skirts? Yer pathetic. Face me like a man."

"I will when ye let Miss Hartley leave."

"I'm not going anywhere."

Duncan swore internally. He didn't know how this was

going to end with his uncle, though he was certain that some type of fight would occur. He didn't want Miss Hartley caught up in any danger that was to come.

"What are ye going tae do, Duncan?" Graeme asked condescendingly. He held his arms out wide, *inviting* Duncan to try and fight him.

Silence filled the room, a silence so thick that Duncan nearly yelped when somebody knocked on the study doors.

Graeme angrily called for whoever it was to come in. One of the soldiers entered, eyeing Duncan and Miss Hartley suspiciously.

"There's a man in the courtyard," he informed Graeme. "He says the magistrate is on his way." He paused, clearly nervous about what he had to say next. "He says he has proof that this castle doesn't belong to you and you'll be arrested."

"What are ye talking about?" Graeme snapped. "He's clearly lying." The more he shouted at the soldier, the clearer it was that he was in the wrong. As he was distracted, Duncan tried to edge around his uncle's right side to get to the gun. He hoped that between his anger and the soldier's news, his uncle's attention would be elsewhere, but Duncan wasn't successful.

Graeme wasn't as preoccupied as he'd hoped. As Duncan grabbed the barrel—the closest part to him—his uncle grabbed the lock. They ended up in a struggle, Duncan furiously trying to keep himself out of the way of the muzzle as his uncle fumbled for the trigger. It discharged. They both dropped it in shock.

Miss Hartley screamed, and Duncan ran to her. Nothing else mattered in that moment as he feared she'd been hit. He grabbed her face in his hands. "Are ye hurt?" he repeated frantically.

She didn't answer, simply throwing her arms around his neck. Her breathing was ragged and her heart was racing.

It soon became clear who had been hit. The soldier was slumped against the wall. He clutched his leg, his face pale. The other soldiers rushed in on hearing the gunshot and went straight to the aid of their injured comrade.

"He shot me!" the man cried out indignantly. All faces turned to Graeme, who was staring at the discharged rifle on the floor at his feet. His eyes were wide and his face was pale.

Duncan strode across the room, grabbed the man by his lapels and kicked the rifle into the corner.

He heard Miss Hartley give orders to the soldiers. "Get him to the kitchens. Mr Peters has bandages. Tobias can get a doctor. We need to get everybody else out of here now before anyone else gets hurt."

Duncan turned his wrath on his uncle. "Ye shot someone. Ye could have shot *her!*" Calm, measured behaviour was now a tiny spot in the distance in Duncan's mind. "Ye could have killed her. Is yer hatred of me worth all of this?"

Graeme shook himself out of the stupor created by staring at the gun and laughed. "Ye are the one who fired that rifle, nae me," he argued unconvincingly. "And this isnae because I hate ye. I dunnae care about ye at all. I'm here tae claim ma birth right."

"Ye liar," Duncan seethed, pressing his face even closer to his uncle's. "Ye could have claimed this place years ago. Ye dunnae care about Laird Fraser's legacy. Ye just dunnae want me tae have anything. What is it about me that gets ye so riled?"

Graeme shoved him hard, breaking Duncan's grip on his clothes. Duncan stumbled backwards into Miss Hartley.

"Ye need tae leave," he told her as he steadied himself. Something animal had taken over Graeme — there was no reason left in his eyes.

Duncan barely had time to push her through the door before he launched himself at his uncle, who was reaching for the gun. He grabbed the back of Graeme's coat as the other hand formed a fist that landed a punch on the left of his temple.

"Yer father was pathetic too," Graeme spat as he fought against Duncan, catching him in the jaw with a strong punch. "But everybody loved him best. He was the eldest. He got everything, and I didnae get anything." He punched Duncan again and threw him at the desk by the windows.

"I was the one who courted yer mother first, but she liked him better. Even our own mother preferred him. Then ye came along. His precious wee heir. Ye were the one who'd grow tae inherit everything that *I* deserved."

Duncan, still dizzy from the first punch, tried to block as his uncle took another swing.

"I wasnae sad when yer father died," Graeme taunted. "Ma only regret was that I hadnae killed him before ye were even born. Though it was easy tae turn yer family against ye. Ye were so snivelling and pathetic, it wasnae hard tae convince them the inheritance would be better suited tae me. Yer mother happily signed anything I put in front of her. I would have thrown ye out sooner, but ma stupid mother had tae like ye."

Duncan snapped. He launched himself at his uncle. His shoulder connected with Graeme's chest and he forced him backwards. Graeme's fists beat against his back, trying to force him to let go.

Duncan's momentum carried them across the room, halted only when they hit the wall next to the door. Duncan let go, preparing himself to throw the hardest punch of his life against his uncle's jaw.

He swung, but Graeme caught him. Using Duncan's changing centre of gravity against him, he switched their positions.

With his back against the wall, Duncan had to use his arms

to stop Graeme's hands from contracting around his throat. He leant back and let the wall take his weight as he lifted a leg to kick his uncle in the gut.

Graeme stumbled. Duncan kicked him again, still holding his arms, refusing to let him fall and making the hits more powerful.

"Ye bastard," Duncan yelled finally letting go and watching Graeme drop to the floor. "Ye pathetic, jealous, snivelling worm. Ye killed ma father? And fer what? Nae person respects ye or likes ye any more than they did before, they're just scared of ye."

Graeme wiped a hand across his mouth. "It got me what I wanted," he sneered, unsteadily getting to his feet again.

"Face it, Graeme," Duncan grunted. "Ye've lost. Godshollow isnae yers. It's mine. I have a home and I have a woman who will love me like I deserve. All yer jealous conniving has been fer nothing. I've won. Admit defeat."

"Never." Graeme lunged once more.

Duncan twisted and caught his foot in the crease behind his uncle's knee. He went down but used his other leg to sweep Duncan's feet out from under him. Punches and kicks flew in every direction.

Graeme was the first to regain his feet. He ran to his desk, scrambling for the rifle, desperately trying to find something to load it with.

"With the papers I have, and yer confession, everyone will see ye fer who ye really are." Breathing hard, Duncan advanced on his uncle, trying to reach him before he could reload the rifle. "Everyone will know what ye've done, and it'll prove ma nanna was right all along tae favour ma father."

Graeme roared in anger. His hands worked furiously on the gun as be pulled back the lock and took aim at Duncan.

"I should have killed ye too when I had the chance," he bellowed.

Duncan stopped dead. He was right in the path of the gun—he could try to dodge out of the way of the bullet, but success was unlikely.

He held his breath as he heard the trigger pulled.

Duncan heard an explosion. He closed his eyes and waited.

CHAPTER TWENTY-SEVEN

The room was silent.

Duncan waited for pain to flood his body.

Seconds ticked by. Still no pain.

Cautiously, Duncan opened first one eye and then the other as he took in the scene before him.

Graeme lay in a heap by the desk. The gun, fallen from his grip, lay across his legs. He had found a packet from somewhere, the casing was discarded on the floor next to him, but he must have loaded it wrong. It appeared that the gun had exploded in his face. Wisps of smoke hung in the air, the smell of ignited gunpowder dominating.

Graeme's hands and face were blacked and burnt. His eyes were closed, and his body limp.

Duncan carefully approached him. Slowly he bent down at his uncle's side — Duncan was sure he was dead, but wouldn't put it past him to fake injury to gain the upper hand.

Duncan shook the man's shoulder and tried to feel breath against his hand. There was nothing. The explosion must have killed him instantly.

Duncan stood back up. Looking down at Graeme, he didn't know how to feel. There was no relief. He'd never had any intention of killing his uncle, but he had expected that when he'd defeated Graeme, he would have felt some kind of release of pressure and fear.

This felt like a hollow victory. Duncan wanted Graeme to answer for his crimes, be made to repent and make reparations for his actions. That would never happen now. This wasn't Duncan's idea of justice.

He was drawn from his ruminations by the entrance of Miss Hartley. She threw open the doors and ran to Duncan, wrapping her arms around him. Duncan winced as she pressed against the bruises his uncle had inflicted.

"We heard another shot," she said in a shaking voice. "I feared . . ."

Duncan could see tears swimming in her eyes and knew she couldn't put words to what she'd feared. Despite the pain, he hugged her tight.

"I'm safe, lass," he assured her, though to his own ears, his voice sounded disbelieving more than reassuring. It was a miracle that he was still alive, really. Had Graeme competently loaded the gun, that would have ended very differently.

"It blew up in his face," Duncan explained in a flat voice. He was still trying to come to terms with what had happened for himself, let alone try to explain it to someone else.

Miss Hartley greeted the news with a sombre nod of the head. She too, it seemed, couldn't celebrate this sort of victory.

She looked up at him and reached up her hand, lightly running her fingers over his swollen right eye.

"You need to see a doctor," she told him gently.

Duncan was happy to let her take over the situation and allowed himself to be guided from the room when she took his hand.

A large congregation had gathered in the entrance hall,

Major Hartley stood with Mr Daniels and the magistrate, who was instructing the soldiers' commanding officer, showing him the signed deeds. The man offered a simple salute and went back to his men, who began to make preparations to leave.

It appeared that Mr Daniels had done as he was instructed and had gone to the Luttons. They were by the front doors greeting a newly arrived gentleman. When they saw Duncan and Miss Hartley they rushed over.

Immediately, General Lutton put an arm around Duncan's shoulder and took his weight—Duncan must have looked worse than he realised. He helped Duncan into a seat.

Finally able to rest, Duncan realised just how much pain he was in. He'd taken a severe beating from his uncle, but the energy of the moment had blocked it from him until now.

The gentleman with them hadn't even had a chance to take his hat off when he was pulled over to Duncan. As he removed his top hat, he introduced himself as Doctor Allen. He checked Duncan over, offering what remedies he could from his bag. "Rest, along with a large glass of brandy would be as effective as anything," he offered his opinion. No bones seemed to be broken. Duncan simply needed to rest, not strain anything, and in time the bruises would heal on their own.

When the doctor had gone, Duncan noticed the magistrate coming towards him.

"Where's the other man?" he asked plainly.

"Dead," Duncan replied solemnly. "His gun exploded."

"I'll send for the undertaker." Then the man walked away to converse with a boy who appeared to be his assistant, who it seemed had arrived whilst Duncan was receiving care.

Duncan knew there would be more questions, but it seemed the magistrate was giving him time to rest first, as Duncan wasn't disturbed whilst he sipped the brandy the doctor had recommended. There would be time enough to explain everything that had happened.

Duncan watched the undertaker removed his uncle's body from Godshollow with mixed emotions. He was glad that the war between them was now over, but he could never be happy about the loss of a life.

A few weeks later, he was able, however, to take pleasure from the justice meted out to Mr Ocheridge.

The man had tried to run but had been caught on the road to Gloucester. Once he'd been turned over to the magistrate and incarcerated, he had more than happily given the information asked of him. He had been snivelling and grovelling, making himself out to be the victim. He cried that he'd been coerced and manipulated by Graeme Mackenzie's lies through his letters and should therefore be relieved of any responsibility.

The courts didn't see it that way, as his reasoning was completely farcical. Ocheridge had had every opportunity to check Graeme Mackenzie's statements. He had even had them refuted by Duncan Mackenzie's evidence, but had chosen to continue with his scheme. Clearly the lawyer had acted purely to get the money that was offered and was completely responsible for any actions he took in achieving that goal. He was given a lengthy jail sentence.

For his part in events, Major Hartley too received punishment. Duncan had held his fiancée as she cried for her brother the afternoon he left to re-join the army as a private, taking service to the crown in place of a jail sentence.

It would take a long time for the effects of these events to be overcome for Duncan, for Miss Hartley, for everyone involved. But Duncan knew that the effort to make a new life for himself would be worth it. And he felt incredibly thankful for the astonishing woman who would be by his side.

EPILOGUE: 1822

"Aunty Bee-Bee!"

One-year-old Alfred Hartley toddled on pudgy legs towards Beatrice, sticky fingers reaching for her.

She picked him up and he giggled happily.

"He's grown so much," she commented to Charles.

It had been a tough year for the family. Charles and Annabelle had to be told what had happened, and very soon they were saying goodbye to Jasper before they had even processed what he'd done.

Then there had been the wedding. With his uncle dead, her fiancé had finally inherited his father's legacy. Proving his kind nature, he'd made sure his mother was provided for in Scotland. Beatrice and Duncan had talked at length about inviting her to live with them at Godshollow, but even once Duncan had decided he could put the pain of her collusion with his uncle behind him, his mother had refused the offer. Graeme's poison had done its work, and Judith Mackenzie wanted nothing to do with her son—though she was happy to take his money. As sad as it was, it looked as though Duncan would be better off without his mother in his life.

With that arranged, Duncan and Beatrice were able to begin a new life together, starting with their marriage.

The wedding had been simple. Jasper had already been sent to the army. Charles officiated, and Mr Daniels gave Beatrice away. The only other guests at the service were Annabelle and Alfred, and the Luttons.

The ball they held to mark the occasion, however, included

a large guest list.

Beatrice watched her husband as he stood on the balcony, observing the guests milling about as they waited for the party to officially commence.

Duncan turned and saw her watching him. He smiled and came to her side. "They're ready fer us, *Mo gràidh.*"

She smiled and hugged Alfred. "Back to daddy, sweetheart. Aunty Bee has to talk to all these lovely people."

The toddler put up a little resistance but was talked into going back eventually.

Beatrice walked to the edge of the balcony, hands on the rail and faced the assembled crowd who were lulling into silence.

"I'd like to thank you all very much for coming tonight," she started when the crowd went quiet. "It's an important day for my husband and me, and we are so grateful you could join us." She squeezed Duncan's hand.

"Aye," he agreed. "I want tae thank ye all fer accepting me intae this community. I realise that the circumstances of ma moving here were less than ideal, but I really appreciate yer support."

The crowd gave a gentle applause.

"With that in mind," Beatrice continued, "we would like to welcome you into our home, and we hope that you enjoy the ball."

The applause was louder as the guests realised that meant the dancing, drinking, and card-playing could begin.

Beatrice watched happily as the party began in earnest when the band struck up and began playing happy, energetic music.

Duncan went to join the crowd, but Beatrice held him back.

He gave her a quizzical eyebrow tilt.

Beatrice smiled back and held his hand. "I just want to take it all in for a moment," she told him. "I don't think I've ever been happier, and I want to remember this forever." This was a perfect moment. The house was bustling with activity and joy, and she was here with the people who meant the most to her.

Duncan pulled her to him. "I know what ye mean. This is a wonderful moment, but I promise ye there will be many, many more."

"I'll hold you to that promise."

And she did.

You may also enjoy the following from eXtasy Books Inc:

Godshollow
Catherine Price

Excerpt

"Mrs Evans, this is my niece, Miss Annabelle Knight. Well, she's not exactly my niece. My husband is her maternal uncle. You know what I mean. Anyway, Annabelle is accompanying us to Bath for the season."

"Oh! How wonderful," Mrs Evans cried loudly, turning to her daughters. "Look, girls, how sweet she is. How lovely, look at her curls. Oh, just darling." She didn't pause for breath, reaching out and grabbing a ringlet of Annabelle's hair. Mrs Evans' tone was the kind one might adopt with regard to a small puppy, which, to these large women, was the way Annabelle must have seemed. They were practically as wide as they were tall, and they loomed over Annabelle. The girl let out a small, nervous laugh.

Oblivious to Annabelle's discomfort, the ladies continued with their assessment. Mrs Evans' daughters, who had been tittering behind her, giggled at their mother's appraisal and added their own.

"Just wonderful," said one.

"So darling," chimed in the other. They both regarded Annabelle with the same shrewd eye with which one would appraise cattle at a market.

While the girls had clearly inherited their looks from their mother, from the brown eyes to the light dusting of freckles over their noses, their accents most definitely came from a Welsh father. It was strong and thick. Annabelle had never heard anything like it, and it took her a considerable amount of concentration to discern what they were saying.

Their mother spoke with a softer English accent that was peppered with small Welsh moments, indicating a good amount of time spent in the country. "These are my twins," Mrs Evans announced. "Carys." She gestured to the girl on her left. "And Gwennyth." She motioned to the other. Annabelle wondered how she was going to remember which twin was which. They were identical, even, unhelpfully, down to their choice in clothing. Both girls dutifully curtseyed.

One of them leant forward and added, "Most people just call me Gwen."

Right. Annabelle noted. So Gwen is the one with the beauty spot beside her right eye. She curtseyed again to each girl as she searched for other unique identifiers.

"Don't you just love Bath, Miss Knight?" Carys asked as though she thought every young lady in the world should have an intimate knowledge of the place.

"Actually, this is my first time," Annabelle admitted timorously.

The twins looked at each other in horror.

"Your first time!" Carys exclaimed, completely aghast, her tone bordering on offended.

"We go every year," Gwen continued, shocked.

"It's just the best place."

"Oh, the very best!"

"Especially for eligible young ladies." At this, both girls dissolved into giggles, laughing at their own insinuations.

Annabelle nodded along, though she couldn't truly

empathise. She knew that Bath was, aside from London, the best place for a young woman to be. But her parents had strictly forbidden her to travel there until she attained the age of eighteen because of its less than sparkling reputation.

"I can't believe you've never visited," Carys said contemptuously.

"How is that possible?" Gwen questioned.

Annabelle made the quick assessment that Gwen was definitely the nicer twin. While that didn't help her immediately, knowing that would help her distinguish which one was speaking.

"I've never had the opportunity to go before now," Annabelle replied simply. "It's something I've always wanted to do. I'm very excited to be visiting. I've read everything about it. There are so many things I would like to do while I'm there."

Gwen seemed satisfied with the answer, though Carys looked more sceptical. Suddenly, the sterner twin was seized by an idea, or at least Annabelle hoped she was—that, or she was having a fit. Carys turned to her sister and began to whisper theatrically. More giggling ensued, and they finally faced Annabelle.

"We have decided," one twin—Carys?—said, with much grandeur.

"That, as it's your first time in Bath . . ." the other added.

"And you'll need someone to show you around . . ."

"And we've been many times before . . ."

"We are the best people . . ."

"To take you under our wings . . ."

"And show you how to do Bath." They nodded in unison and eagerly awaited Annabelle's reply.

Annabelle was so confused by all the sentence-sharing and the back and forth that all she could do was smile weakly and say thank you, though she didn't know exactly what she'd agreed to.

"What a clever idea," Mrs Evans exclaimed, reminding the

young girls of her existence. "Don't you think, Moira?"

"Marvellous." Mrs Daniels nodded. "Of course, Colin and I know the area substantially," she added quickly. "We know it better than anyone, but I'm sure Annabelle would prefer some younger companions to keep her company. Though, of course, she adores us. Don't you dear?"

Annabelle nodded vigorously. Her aunt didn't like to be contradicted and hated even the remotest implication that she wasn't the best at everything.

"Well then, it's settled," Mrs Evans beamed. "Girls, tell Miss Annabelle about the ball."

In the deserted inn, it wasn't difficult for the young ladies to find an empty table. Once they were sat down, Gwen began to tell Annabelle about the upcoming event.

"Oh, it is the best ball," she announced, her boundless enthusiasm giving away her identity. "They have it every year and it is the most wonderful thing. There's tea, and dancing, and card tables, and so many eligible bachelors." Gwen began to giggle girlishly then stopped suddenly. "I know!" she declared. "We must all get ready for it together. Where are you staying? You may be closer than we are."

"I think my uncle said it was St James' Square," Annabelle replied when Gwen stopped to draw breath.

Carys looked disdainful. "Hmm . . ." She paused, her nose turning up at the thought. "It is closer to the ballrooms, but I'm sure it's nowhere near as comfortable as our accommodation in Sidney Place."

Annabelle quickly decided that arguing with Carys would be a bad choice and instead nodded her head in agreement. "I'm sure." she said sweetly. "But we risk less damage to our dresses if we are closer to the halls."

Gwen's head bobbed enthusiastically. "Quite so. And" — she spun on her toes to face Carys — "St James' Square is rather lovely."

The other twin gave no response to this. Instead, she raked her gaze over Annabelle's appearance. "What will you wear?" she asked in a belittling tone.

"Well, I have one dress that's my favourite. I've worn it for years," Annabelle replied fondly. "It's yellow with—"

"That will never do," Carys cut in harshly. "This is the ball of the season, you know. You can't go in wearing old clothes!" She said this with such a tone one would have thought Annabelle had suggested she would make an appearance wearing just her under-things.

Annabelle was too stunned to make an intelligible reply. Luckily, she was saved from having to find a rebuttal by the arrival of Mr Daniels.

"There you two are. I've been searching for you. Bath is still a fair way away, and we really should get going."

Annabelle nodded and rose from the table, happy to escape this odd, insulting conversation. As she left, Carys fired her parting shot.

"Don't worry," the Welsh girl called out. "We'll look through your clothes to find the least terrible gown. And if there's nothing suitable, I'm sure Gwen has something you can borrow."

Annabelle curtseyed politely and followed her uncle out of the room, trying to stop the flush she felt rising in her cheeks. She sat in solitary embarrassment whilst her aunt bid farewell to Mrs Evans and they made plans to meet for lunch the next day.

Annabelle waved from the carriage as the Evanses shrank into the distance, but as she sat back in her seat, once they'd completely disappeared, she wondered just exactly what her aunt's introductions had gotten her into.

ABOUT THE AUTHOR

Catherine Price lives just outside of Bath, UK, and has a love of 18th and 19th Century history.

She has two degrees in History and Heritage Studies which she uses to lend authenticity to her novels.

She is also the creator and host of The Addicted Austenite Podcast, with weekly episodes that cover everything to do with Jane Austen.